"Ready?" Grant grasped the knob as Rena squared her shoulders.

"Ready as I'll ever be

Grant opened the do
she was.

Our Rosie.

Grant squatted down to her height. "Hey there, kiddo," he said.

Rosie looked at each of them in turn, as a slow smile lit up her face. Grant held out his arms, and Rosie ran to him. "Daddy, Daddy, oh, Daddy..."

Through her tears, Rena could see that Grant's eyes were moist, too.

"Ah, my sweet Rosie-girl," he said, holding her at arm's length. "Let me look at you." Bracketing her face with his big, strong hands, he stared into her eyes. "I'm so happy to see you!"

"I'm happy to see you, too!"

He turned slightly, held out a hand to invite Rena closer. "Go ahead, sweetie, give your mom a big hello hug."

Oh, how it hurt that Rosie only moved closer because of Grant's gentle nudge! Rena wrapped her arms around her daughter, willing herself to appreciate the momentary contact, to ignore the way Rosie stood, arms pressed tight to her sides, stiff as a statue.

Rena turned her loose and feigned a smile. Hands on the tiny shoulders, she said, "I missed you, sweet girl, missed you so much!"

The child's blank stare shook her to the core.

Dear Reader,

I'm sure that every time you hear about a missing child, your heart breaks a little, just as mine does. Our instinct is to protect the little ones, so we put our faith in first responders, search and rescue personnel and their well-trained dogs...and God. Our grief is palpable when the worst-possible scenario unfolds, but we're overjoyed when parents are reunited with their child.

Such is the story of Rena and Grant VanMeter, whose little girl was kidnapped at age three. Imagine their grief, compounded by the separation that seemed their only avenue to respite.

Then, five years later, the lead detective calls to say "We found her!", upending their world yet again as they reunite...for Rosie's sake.

Through hard work, acceptance and forgiveness, Rena and Grant realize the love that brought them together in the first place is still very much alive, and as the family heals, their future looks promising. Sadly, that isn't the case for too many of the families that experience similar shattering losses. (Case in point: the family whose story served as my inspiration for *Bringing Rosie Home*.)

My prayer for all missing children is that they will return, safe and unharmed, to the loving arms of their parents. I pray just as hard for fractured families that never find their way back to shared happiness. And I pray that none of us will ever be touched by such searing pain.

Wishing you well in all you do,

Loree

HEARTWARMING

Bringing Rosie Home

—

Loree Lough

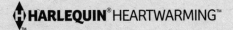

Recycling programs
for this product may
not exist in your area.

ISBN-13: 978-1-335-63348-4

Bringing Rosie Home

Copyright © 2018 by Loree Lough

Printed in U.S.A.

www.Harlequin.com

Loree Lough once sang for her supper. That space reserved in pubs for "the piano lady"? Well, that's where she sat, strumming her Yamaha in cities all over the United States and Canada. Now and then, she blows the dust from the old six-string to croon a tune or two, but mostly, she writes. She feels blessed that most of her stories have earned four- and five-star reviews, but what Loree is most proud of are her Readers' Choice awards.

Loree and her husband live in a Baltimore suburb and enjoy spending time at their cozy cabin in Pennsylvania's Allegheny Mountains (where she has *nearly* perfected her critter-tracking skills). They have two lovely daughters and seven "grandorables," and because she believes in giving back, Loree donates generously to charity (see the full list at www.loreelough.com).

Loree *loves* hearing from her readers, some of whom have become lifelong friends! Find her on Facebook, Twitter or Pinterest.

Books by Loree Lough

Harlequin Heartwarming

By Way of the Lighthouse

The Man She Knew

Those Marshall Boys

Once a Marine
Sweet Mountain Rancher
The Firefighter's Refrain

A Child to Love

Raising Connor
Devoted to Drew
Saving Alyssa

For more books by Loree Lough, check out Harlequin.com.

This story is dedicated to those whose loved ones have gone missing, and to the once-missing individuals who have been found. May they all know the comfort and peace of *home*, wherever they are.

ACKNOWLEDGMENTS

Huge and heartfelt thanks to all those who provided insights, opinions and information that helped lend authenticity to this story: the helpful employees of Baltimore's Child Protective Services office, FBI agents Donald McCarthy and Paul Reagan*, pediatric psychiatrists Ron Abrams and Sue Robinson, detective Jack Royer, Adele and Phil Morrison* (whose son went missing in 1995), and Donna Ryan*, whose once-missing daughter was returned to her loving arms in 2001. (* = names changed at individuals' request.)

CHAPTER ONE

AS SHE'D DRESSED this morning, Rena had decided this would be her last session with Dr. Hutchinson. Two years of therapy, and what did she have to show for it? A smaller bank account and dozens of wasted hours, that was what. And the psychologist hadn't brought her little girl back. Or saved Rena's marriage.

But the analyst surprised her, shifting her line of questioning from Rosie's kidnapping to Rena's relationship—or lack thereof.

"How are things with Grant?" Martha asked.

They'd been separated over three years now, ever since Rena had taken her mother-in-law's advice and turned Rosie's room into a home office for Grant. When he saw it, every ugly thought and accusation he'd kept to himself had poured out, and when Rena had realized it was her presence—not sparkly tiaras, dolls and Teddy bears—that reminded him of that awful day, she'd offered to leave.

And he'd done nothing to stop her.

"We haven't spoken in months." Not since his grandfather died and he'd called to ask if she wanted to attend the services.

"Do you ever regret leaving?"

Only every day! Yes, Grant had allowed bitterness and blame to turn him into a surly, brooding man, but Rena remembered well the man he'd once been. The man he'd still be if she hadn't taken her eyes off Rosie that day at the zoo.

"It was the right thing to do," she said.

"For Grant? Or for you?"

"Both of us. Living under the same roof with the person responsible for what happened to Rosie… I don't blame him for anything."

Rena held her breath, partly to keep from remembering how it felt to have her sweet little girl beside her one minute and gone the next.

"We were both miserable."

"Still," Martha injected, "I wish he'd consider seeing someone. It might help him come to terms with it, and admit, finally, that it wasn't your fault. That it could have happened to anyone."

They'd been over this a dozen times. Maybe more. Rena didn't feel much like repeating that she'd go to her grave feeling guilty for taking her eyes off Rosie during the field trip.

"But it didn't happen to anyone. It happened to Rosie, because of *me*."

Martha sighed. "I think you know what I'm going to say to that…"

Rena was about to admit that yes, she knew, and that pretending she wasn't to blame only made it hurt more. But her cell phone buzzed.

Rena glanced at the number.

"Sorry, but I have to take this. It's my… It's Grant. Our hour is almost up, anyway, so…"

Rena was almost out the door before Martha said, "See you next week."

No, she wouldn't. But there wasn't time to

get into that now. Later, she'd call and cancel all future appointments.

"Hello?"

"Rena. I have important news. Are you sitting down?"

His voice sounded hoarse, deeper than usual. When she'd spoken with his mom a few days ago, Tina had complained about a dizzy spell. Grant was aware that she and his mother had stayed in close contact, and to his credit, had never said or done anything to discourage it.

"Is Tina all right?"

"She's fine. Sends her love."

Rena exhaled a breath of relief. She cared about her mother-in-law almost as much as her own mother. But if he hadn't called about Tina's health…

"Heard from Burt Campbell this morning."

The detective who'd been assigned to the kidnapping case before FBI Agent Gonzalez had stepped in. Heart pounding, she made her way to the nearest bench and sat down. A call from Campbell could mean just one thing: after all this time, they'd finally found her little girl's body.

"He got a call from the Chicago police." Grant cleared his throat. "They've found Rosie. Alive."

CHAPTER TWO

WHAT A CRUEL joke it would be if it was someone else's little girl.

"Are they... How can they be sure it's Rosie?"

"She gave them our names," Grant said. "Our address. Her preschool teacher's name. Told them she called her favorite Teddy bear, Mr. Fuzzbottom. They sent me pictures, too. I'll forward them to your cell. It's our Rosie. No doubt in my mind."

Our Rosie... She hadn't heard him use that phrase since—

"I'll make reservations and let you know when our flight takes off." He paused. Cleared his throat. "If you want to come with me to Chicago, that is."

"Of course I want to!"

Another pause, long enough this time that

she was about to check if the call had been dropped.

"I'll go home right now, dig up the paperwork. Rosie's birth certificate. Her immunization records. Photographs. Our passports…"

Rena had left so quickly that day, more than three years ago now, that she hadn't even thought to grab her birth certificate and passport. But the Chicago police would need proof that she and Grant were who they claimed to be.

"Rosie is speaking with a pediatric psychiatrist now," Grant continued. "By the time we get there—I'm thinking midafternoon tomorrow at the latest—she'll be prepared for the fact that we're coming to take her home."

Home. The house they'd shared since the day after their honeymoon, and the only place Rosie had ever lived…until the abduction. And where accusations and arguments pushed Grant and Rena apart even before she moved to Delaware's Fenwick Island.

"I, ah, I think for the time being you should plan to stay at the house. Maybe you can stop by tonight, before we leave for Chicago, so you can unpack, make it look like you never left. Spend the night. That way, just one car to worry about at the airport."

It was a lot to absorb in just a few minutes. She couldn't imagine living under the same roof with him again, not after all the harsh words they'd exchanged. But there would be plenty of time later to question his decision. Right now, he was waiting for her reply.

"All right. I'll go straight home to pack and make arrangements with work. And find someone to water my plants. And collect my mail. And then it'll take me a few hours to drive to Ellicott City. Unless there's traffic, I can be there by six."

"Rena, you know what this means…"

"That we have to put on a good front, make Rosie believe we're still a happy couple."

"Exactly. She doesn't need to cope with her parents' breakup on top of everything else she's gone through."

How many times had she wondered about that? A thousand? Ten thousand? Even after accepting that they might never know, Rena had always hoped the kidnapper had been gentle and kind.

"I…I think that's best, too," she told him. "Anything, *any*thing for Rosie's sake."

"I'll pull something together for supper. We can talk about how we're going to proceed while we eat."

The invitation was a big sacrifice on his part, especially considering that during their last months together in the house, she'd slept in the guest room. He hadn't stopped her from doing that, either. Would they go back to living as roommates? Rena couldn't imagine a more uncomfortable scenario.

"Yes, yes, that's a good idea."

Did she sound as much like a robot to Grant as she did to herself?

"How have you been, by the way?"

It surprised her that he'd bothered to ask. "Fine." *Seeing a shrink, trying not to give in to insanity, dealing with insomnia, but…* "And you?"

"Fine," he echoed.

But she knew he wasn't. She could hear it

in his strained voice. Neither of them were fine. How could they be?

"Well, I'd better skedaddle."

How long since she'd heard him recite the phrase that had so often inspired good-natured teasing between them? Not once in the five years since Rosie vanished, like the smoke from a spent match. It told her that Grant had hope, real hope, for the first time since the kidnapping. His belief that they'd find her had been the second biggest issue between them next to the blame. The third biggest? Her dreams of having another baby. *"Another child won't replace Rosie. How can you just give up on her?"* he'd demand. *"What kind of mother just throws in the towel this way?"*

"Just so you know, I asked Mom not to come around for a few days, to give Rosie time to adjust to being back," Grant said now.

Rena clenched her jaw. "But Grant, your mother was always such a huge part of her life. Wouldn't it seem strange to her if Tina didn't stop by once we're..." She couldn't bring herself to call it home. Not yet. "At least for a little while?"

He didn't reply right away, and Rena braced herself for his dismissal.

"You're right, I guess," he said, surprising her. "I'll give her a call. You think she should be at the house, waiting? Or stop by a couple of hours after we get home?"

Who was this cordial man? In their last few months of living together, he hadn't agreed with her on anything.

"Later, maybe, to give Rosie a chance to look around, reacquaint herself with her surroundings." *And being with us.*

"Right. Right."

In the moment of silence that followed, she considered asking how the news had affected him. But she wasn't quite ready to go there with him yet. For now, cordial felt like the safest course of action.

"I'd better let you go. You still have your house keys?"

"Yes…" But even if she didn't, Rena could use the one she'd hidden in the ceramic frog lawn ornament near the front door. Unless a storm had blown it from the table, she was sure it would still be there.

"Good. If I'm not there, let yourself in. Nothing has changed, so you won't have any trouble finding things. Just make yourself at home."

"Thanks, Grant."

"That isn't exactly true…that nothing has changed," he continued. "Rosie's room is different from when you last saw it."

"Oh?"

"I found all her stuff in the attic, right where you put it, and thanks to those pictures you took for the insurance album, everything is back to the way it was before…"

His voice trailed off, but she knew what he'd stopped himself from saying: *Before you packed things up. Put our girl out of sight, out of mind.*

"I…ah… Drive safely, Rena," he said, and hung up.

She sat in Martha's waiting room, still as a statue, as tears filled her eyes. By this time tomorrow, she'd get to hold her sweet daughter in her arms again. Rosie was alive. *Rosie was alive!*

"Must have been some phone call," her therapist said, poking her head out of her office.

Rena knuckled her damp eyes. "It was Grant. He said…he said they…they found Rosie."

Martha walked over and sat beside her, sliding an arm across Rena's shoulders.

"Oh, Rena, that's wonderful news!"

"She's in Chicago. I don't know any of the details. Except that Rosie is talking to a child specialist right now, so that by the time we arrive, she'll be somewhat prepared. We decided to present a united front. I'm moving back into the house to make the transition easier for her."

"Grant's idea, or yours?"

"His, but I agree."

Leaning back slightly, Martha said, "That's a lot for him to ask, don't you think, after the way he treated you?"

"I'm not fooling myself. I know it won't be easy, especially not at first, but I'll do whatever it takes to help Rosie adjust to being home again. It's the least I can do after…"

Martha held up a hand, effectively silencing the self-deprecating comment that would follow. "How old is she now?"

"She turned nine three weeks ago, on May 5."

"And she was three when she was taken?"

"Almost four."

Martha pointed out that Rosie had no doubt changed a lot in all that time. "Are you ready for that?"

"I haven't really had time to wrap my mind around the news yet. But thankfully, I'll have hours and hours to think about it." During the drive to Ellicott City. On the plane to Chicago. And of course, tonight, after she retreated to the guest room...

"I was heading home, but I can stay if you want to talk."

Rena got to her feet. "Thanks, but I need to get home and pack for the drive to Maryland."

Martha stood, too. "Things are happening fast. If you need me, just call."

Nodding, Rena dropped her phone into her purse and started for the exit. "Thanks," she said. Martha wouldn't hear from her again, but this wasn't the time or place to discuss why. "That's nice to know."

GRANT HADN'T REALIZED how much he'd missed the sound of her voice. Even with the shock of hearing this news, Rena had been calm and quiet. One of the things he'd admired most about her had been her ability to maintain her composure, even during the most stressful moments.

Like the time Rosie fell off the swing and broke her arm. He'd totally freaked out, but Rena had kept her cool and orchestrated a trip to the ER for X-rays, told jokes and made silly faces while the tech set the bone and wrapped Rosie's arm in a cast. And the day he'd nearly electrocuted himself trying to add a circuit breaker to the electrical panel. He'd thought surely he'd bought a one-way ticket to heaven, but her soft, reassuring voice was all it had taken to make him believe he'd be fine.

Fine. It was what she said when he'd asked how she was, and what he'd said when she returned the question. In truth, he'd only felt this frazzled on one other occasion: the day Rosie went missing.

Because Rena had been paying more attention to somebody else's kid than to their little girl.

He felt a little crazy, waffling between loving her still and despising her for putting them in the middle of every parent's worst nightmare.

In all fairness, he hadn't suffered that nightmare alone. Guilt had tormented Rena, turning her from a confident, lively young mother into a jumpy, sleep-deprived woman who burst into tears at the drop of a hat. And he hadn't made things easier for her.

But then, was it his fault that the only reason the nightmare began was because she'd been too busy minding Rosie's classmate to notice a stranger carrying their only child away?

Grant looked at the clock. She'd be here in an hour, two at most. Not much time to get his head straight. And he'd need a clear mind to cope with having her home again. Why in the world had he suggested that she spend the night? *Anything, anything for*

Rosie, she'd said. Still, tonight it would just be the two of them, alone for the first time in three long years.

Shaking his head, he headed to the guest room. Last time he'd checked, there were clean sheets on the bed. Other than a little dust on the furniture, things looked fine. He put a stack of fresh towels in the guest bath, then ran a dust rag over the headboard and footboard, the dresser and night stand.

"Might as well vacuum the family room, too," he muttered, heading for the linen closet. And while he was at it, Grant would figure out what to make for supper.

Tonight would be a cakewalk compared to tomorrow. Hopefully tidying up and preparing the meal would get his mind off... everything.

Such as what she'd look like now? Taller. Weightier. Had the kidnapper cut her hair? Dyed it to ensure no one would recognize her from the photos that had flashed on every TV news broadcast, nationwide? What had the abductor put his little girl through?

Don't go there, he told himself. Because thoughts like that would only make him more angry and resentful of Rena. He was determined to behave like a gentleman tonight. Tomorrow, too. And every day until Rosie had grown fully accustomed to her new life. No matter how long it took.

She'd remembered her address and phone number. His full name and Rena's. Did she remember how much she'd been loved and treasured, too? He hoped so, because that would go a long way to assuring a quick shift from her life in Chicago to life in their peaceful Baltimore suburb.

None of it would be necessary if Rena hadn't dropped the ball that day. *What kind of mother...*

But he'd been down that road a couple hundred times, and all he had to show for it was an overblown resentment of his wife.

How did he expect to share a meal, the house, day-to-day *life* with the woman who'd upended his whole world?

Grant didn't know.

But for Rosie's sake, he intended to try.

CHAPTER THREE

RENA HAD NO way of knowing how long she'd be gone, so she packed a colorful cloth carry-on bag for the trip to Chicago, and a huge suitcase of clothes to stow at the house. She slipped her laptop and e-reader into her briefcase, too, since chances were good that conversation between her and Grant would be severely limited once Rosie was tucked in each night. Her boss at the hospital had been more than understanding, and promised that there would be a job waiting for her whenever she returned.

She turned from 146th Street onto Coastal Highway, hoping her neighbor wouldn't assign the plant-watering, mail-gathering chore to her teenage son. Being greeted by dead philodendrons and late notices sure wouldn't make returning any easier.

Rena glanced into the rearview mirror

and saw the eighty-foot, conical Fenwick Island lighthouse. The beacon had guided many sailors safely to shore and should have been a symbol of safe harbor. Instead, it had always reminded Rena of the separation between her and Grant.

Her cell phone chirped as she merged onto Highway 404.

"Rena," Grant said when she answered. "Where are you?"

"I should be there in about an hour. Why? Did you have trouble booking the flight?"

"No. But it's not for tomorrow anymore. It's tonight. I figured the sooner we arrive, the sooner we can get our girl home again. Booked us a room at the Hilton, too, walking distance from the FBI office."

"Makes sense," she agreed, even though the prospect of sharing a hotel room with him did nothing to calm her nerves. "What about the return flight?"

"We don't know how much red tape we'll have to cut through, so we can book that when we get the go-ahead."

That made sense, too.

"What time is the flight?"

"Midnight. We won't get much sleep to-night—"

She started to say that seeing Rosie for the first time in all these years pretty much guaranteed it. But a new fear rose up, choking off her words: What if Rosie shared Grant's opinion of her? What if she, too, blamed Rena for the kidnapping? Heart pounding, she bit her lower lip and willed herself not to cry.

"I got us a room with two double beds and a roll-away for Rosie, just in case we can't get an early flight out day after tomorrow. Reserved a rental car, too."

He'd thought of everything. Except saying, "I forgive you" or "We're gonna be all right."

What would the three of them talk about? With any luck, the specialist they'd called in to prepare Rosie could provide the answer to that. Something told Rena the doctor would suggest avoiding topics like where Rosie had lived. How she'd lived. But that didn't stop Rena from wondering. Had she gone to school? Did she have friends? Or had the kidnapper held her in seclusion to protect herself?

"What's wrong?" Grant wanted to know.

"Nothing, really. Just…so many questions swirling in my head."

"Yeah, I hear ya. But I'm sure the shrink will give us some guidance. And once we get home, we'll find her a specialist nearby."

"Yes, she'll need all the help she can get. Who knows what sort of things she's been exposed to, things she'll need help putting into perspective."

"We'll all need all the help we can get."

"I'd better go. Traffic is building."

"And it's against the law to talk on your cell phone while driving."

She didn't bother to point out that he'd called her, not the other way around.

"Well, I need to pick up a few things for the trip," he said. "See you soon."

With that, he hung up. She could picture him, pausing, hand on the receiver as he eased it into the cradle. He'd probably chosen something casual to wear after changing out of his for-work-only suit and tie. A Henley shirt, maybe, with snug jeans and Dockers. She'd seen more handsome men on TV and at the movies, but Grant's attractiveness came more from the way he carried and conducted himself than facial features—which were, to be fair, quite striking. Dark-lashed, larger-than-average blue eyes, a broad chin, high cheekbones, and a boyish dimple that showed when he smiled…

She caught herself smiling longingly at the image and cleared her throat. "Stop it, you ninny. Just stop it, right now."

Rena pictured Rosie, too, a much smaller, more feminine version of her dad. They'd been close. So close, in fact, that from time to time, Rena had to shrug off jealousy that her little girl seemed to prefer Grant to her. No surprise, really, when he'd do just about anything to make her giggle, even if it meant acting like a big goofball, himself. Rena had tried making silly faces and noises and adopting comical postures, but couldn't quite pull it off. Grant hadn't minded spending hours in the backyard, either, pushing her on the swing or digging in the sandbox. She remembered Rosie's last Christmas Eve at home, when Grant tucked her in for the night…wearing a dozen colorful plastic barrettes in his hair.

Oh, he had his faults, to be sure. His tendency to make snap judgements about people, for example, and that *way* he had of slurping soup and the milk from his cereal bowl. But he'd been a loving, devoted father. A good and loving husband, too.

For his sake, Rena hoped Rosie would pick up where she'd left off, leaping into his arms at first sight of him, climbing into his lap with one of her favorite storybooks, taking his hand to lead him to her latest castle, made from alphabet blocks.

For her sake? She hoped the child wouldn't hate her for—as Grant had put it—taking her eye off the ball.

Rena had been so lost in thought that she almost missed the exit to Route 50. Slowing to follow the ramp, she estimated her time of arrival: forty minutes, tops. With any luck, Grant would still be out running errands because she wanted a chance to unpack—and peek into every room—while he was gone.

She ran down the short list of things they'd discuss over supper: how long it would take the authorities to verify IDs; what to say to Rosie during those first, all-important moments; whether or not to embrace her.

Grant hadn't given her any details—where they'd found Rosie, for starters—but then, Rena had been so shocked at the news that she hadn't thought to ask. Had she escaped, or had the kidnapper grown tired of caring for her? God willing, the parting hadn't been too traumatic.

Finally, the big green exit sign to Ellicott City came into view.

Finally? What was she thinking? In five minutes, she'd arrive at the house. The one she and Grant had bought together because she'd fallen in love with the white wrap-around porch and he'd dreamed of growing a vegetable garden in the backyard. They'd brought Rosie there when she was barely three days old. It was where they'd celebrated birthdays and Thanksgivings and Christmases, surrounded by Grant's family and hers. And where they'd enjoyed quiet country breakfasts, just the three of them, for no reason other than that Grant and Rosie loved scrapple and pancakes.

Rena made a snap decision to stop at the grocery store just up the road from the house. Grant probably hadn't had time to pick up the ingredients for an old-fashioned morning meal. But Rosie would feel at home sooner if they went right back to doing what they'd done before she was taken.

When she turned into the driveway fifteen minutes later, Rena saw Grant, arms laden with grocery bags. She parked beside his car, taking care not to ding his still-open passenger door.

"Need a hand with that?" she asked.

"Nah. I've got it." He started up the front porch steps. "You made pretty good time."

She tried to read his face, searching for proof that he wasn't happy to see her. She saw none, but he didn't seem ecstatic, either. Popping the trunk, she retrieved her own bags containing Rosie's favorite snacks, microwave popcorn, juice and the breakfast ingredients.

The breath caught in Rena's throat as she followed Grant inside. He hadn't been exaggerating when he'd said nothing had changed. He preferred sleek, modern designs, but he'd stuck with her cross between traditional and rustic style.

"You didn't need to bring food," he said.

"Oh, this is mostly stuff for a big country breakfast. I thought…I thought maybe… maybe on the first morning she's with us…"

He raised one dark eyebrow, highlighting worry lines that hadn't been nearly as deep at his grandfather's funeral. His almost-friendly expression surprised her, and told her that he, too, remembered how much Rosie loved choosing item after item from the food-laden table.

"Ah-ha. Good idea," he said. "Thanks."

He didn't need to thank her, as though she was an ordinary guest in his home who'd offered to help with the dishes. Making Rosie feel at home was just as important to her as it was to him!

Better get used to feeling this way, she thought, hanging her jacket on the back of a kitchen chair.

Rena began putting things away, starting with the bags Grant had dropped onto the table. She had no trouble finding places for everything because, as he'd said, nothing had changed.

Three feet separated the granite-topped island from the pantry, not a lot of space for two people to maneuver. Especially not two people married in name only for so many months. Following a near-collision, Rena expelled a nervous laugh.

Grant, on the other hand, seemed not to find any humor in their predicament. He put down the package of oatmeal he'd been holding and stepped aside.

"Is your trunk still open?"

She felt silly admitting it, even though the neighborhood had never been known for burglaries.

"I'll grab your bags, then," he said, "and put them upstairs."

When he returned to the kitchen, Grant said, "I'll be in the family room. I have to find something to carry all the paperwork in."

"I brought my briefcase." She gestured to where it hung beside her jacket. "Feel free to tuck things in it."

The eyebrow rose again, telling her he had

no intention of going into what might as well be her purse, not even with her permission.

"I'll just stack the paperwork," he said. "You can put it away later."

The tension in here is so thick, you could cut it with a knife, she thought.

Better get used to it. And she'd better figure out how to hide her discomfort from Rosie, because even as a toddler, she'd been sensitive enough to sense when one of her parents had had a bad day.

"Mind if I scout out the house, reacquaint myself with the layout and where things are?"

"Be my guest," he said, closing the back door behind him.

Guest. That was how he saw her, and it hadn't been difficult at all for him to say so, flat out.

There couldn't have been time for Grant to clean the entire house in preparation for her arrival. *Old habits die hard*, she thought, surveying each tidy room. The sages weren't kidding when they said, "Once a marine, always a marine."

Rena left Rosie's room for last, and as she

stepped through the door, her heart pounded. The walls Rena had painted pale gray when she'd turned the room into Grant's office were lavender again—Rosie's favorite color. At least it had been. Would she still like it? Mr. Fuzzbottom leaned against ruffled pillows on the bed. Rena picked up the bear and held on tight.

Grant's attention to detail was amazing, from the location of each stuffed rabbit, puppy and kitten on the bookshelf to the tiny toy chest with *Property of Princess Rosie* stenciled on its lid. She peeked inside it and saw pint-sized train cars, musical instruments and bright-colored building blocks. Rosie was too old for the toys now, and it made Rena wonder about the clothes she'd packed up.

The bureau stood in the same spot beside the door, but its drawers were empty. So was the closet. Rosie had opinions about her clothes, sometimes strong opinions, Rena recalled fondly, and insisted on helping choose replacements when she outgrew sneakers, snowsuits and sweaters. What would she wear tomorrow and the next day? It wasn't like they could just buckle her into the car seat, take her to the mall and—

They didn't have a booster seat suitable for a child her size. How would they get her safely from place to place until they brought her home again?

Overwhelmed by it all, Rena clutched Mr. Fuzzbottom tighter, sank to her knees and gave in to the tears. Rosie had no doubt grown and changed in every imaginable way in the years she'd been with her abductor. Would she even recognize her mom and dad?

"What have I done?" she whispered, sitting on her heels. "What. Have. I. *Done?*"

"Rena?"

Grant squatted beside her, looking concerned. He placed a hand on her forearm.

"I'm…I'm all right," she said, swiping angrily at the traitorous tears. "It's just…" She pointed into the room. "It's just…it's just seeing all this after so long…"

He helped her to her feet and she put the bear back where she'd found it.

"You did a wonderful job in here," she admitted. "Maybe a little too wonderful."

Standing beside her, Grant nodded. "Think she'll still want us to sit in the window seat and read to her? It'll be a tighter squeeze, now, but…"

"Or kneel on either side of her as she says her bedtime prayers?"

Grant exhaled a shaky sigh and pointed toward the dainty hall tree in the corner. "Remember when you sewed her that tutu, for her first dance performance?"

"She hovered like a mother hen the entire time I worked on it…"

"…to make sure you didn't forget to add the sparkles at the hem."

"She's probably outgrown that little table, too, where she hosted tea parties for us and her dolls."

"We'll get her a bigger one. A bigger tea service, too…if she hasn't outgrown her love of tea parties…"

"I have a confession to make, Grant," Rena said softly.

For the first time since joining her in the room, he met her eyes.

"Oh?"

"When I changed everything and you saw

it for the first time, your mom told you I did it for your sake. 'Get rid of all the reminders, so he can adjust once and for all.'"

"I remember."

And from the look on his face, it wasn't a pleasant memory.

"Truth was—*is*—I was only too happy to pack up the things that were such stark reminders of…of what happened."

"I know."

She looked up at him. "You do?"

"Mom told me, the afternoon you left." He focused on Mr. Fuzzbottom. "Then she told me to go after you."

Rena waited, hoping he'd explain why he hadn't followed her. Then again, perhaps she didn't want to hear him repeat all the angry, hurtful things he'd said that day.

"I should never have left you. If I'd stayed, maybe we could have—"

"Let's not go there, okay? It'll be tough enough making this work without dredging up ugly ghosts." Grim-faced and gruff-voiced, he added, "Your stuff is still in the guest room. I thought you might need something from the big suitcase for tonight. You didn't take much with you when you left, and I haven't gotten around to packing up your clothes, yet, so feel free to add what's in your suitcase to the stuff in your closet and drawers."

Any "welcome home" his suggestion might have held was doused when he added that stern *yet*. And it made Rena realize that Grant—perhaps subconsciously—really did see her as a guest in his house. She needed to put a stop to that now, not later.

"I think I'll leave that chore for the time being and fix us something to eat, instead. That'll give you time to gather up all the paperwork you were talking about earlier."

"But I was planning on making us grilled cheese sandwiches with macaroni and cheese and tomato soup."

One of her favorite quick-fix meals. A gesture of kindness?

"Who knows how many days they'll keep us in Chicago," she said. "We'll be eating deli and fast food for the duration. I'll whip up something more substantial and healthy." She took note of his who-do-you-think-you-are expression and added, "You said I should make myself at home…"

"Fine," he said. "I'll be in the family room. Holler when it's ready."

Rena watched him walk away, the way he had when she announced her plan to leave. She didn't think it was possible to hurt him that way again. She'd been wrong.

CHAPTER FOUR

"THE CHICKEN IS DELICIOUS. I haven't had it made this way since…"

He trailed off, and Rena must have sensed his discomfort. "Since I left? I imagine you've shared more than a few meals with Tina in the past few years."

He'd given her that opening. *Shouldn't have dredged up the past. Not even the good stuff.*

Rena sat back. "I should have called her, invited her to supper."

"I'm glad you didn't. You and I have stuff to hash out." Too much honesty, too soon? Grant wondered. He cleared his throat. "Besides, she's at Muriel's tonight."

"Oh, that's right. This is Tuesday, her bridge night." Rena ran a fingertip around the rim of her wineglass. "I think it's great that she's still doing all the things that bring her so much pleasure."

Was that a hint for him to take a lesson from his mom, step out and live life to its fullest, even after the loss of a loved one? He took a bite of buttered wild rice to stop himself from saying something rash. Did she feel that way because *she'd* moved forward? Had she left a guy behind on Fenwick Island?

He'd tried dating a time or two, nice women he'd met through coworkers, and blind dates set up by former frat brothers. But because he and Rena had never pursued a divorce, being with another woman always felt just plain *wrong*. Plus, despite everything, he loved Rena, and probably always would. He'd always blame her, too, for what happened to Rosie. And since the blame outweighed the love—

"So do you think Rosie will have questions for us?" Rena asked.

For you, *maybe,* he thought, since Rena had been the reason the kidnapper had succeeded in the first place.

"She must. I know *I* have a thousand questions," she pressed on.

Grant lifted his glass to his lips. "Such as?"

"Such as where she went to school. *If* she went to school. What sort of house she lived in. Were there other children? Did they feed her healthy meals? Did she see a pediatrician regularly, and is she up to date on all her immunizations? And if she did, how did the kidnapper hide the truth from the doctor, from the principal and teachers, from neighbors and friends and fam—"

"I'm sure the psychiatrist will fill us in on all that." During their phone call, he'd told her what the agent said. An abbreviated version of the facts, but enough information to give her the gist of things. Maybe, under the stress of it all, she'd forgotten. "She was found wandering alone in a mall, remember, after that…that woman died of an aneurism?"

Rena nodded. "Yes. I remember. But…" She waved a hand in front of her face. "Oh, I know she'll be taller—of *course* she'll be taller. She's nine years old. And naturally, she'll weigh more, too. But—and I know this might sound silly—but does she still have all that beautiful, long blond hair? Did they cut it or dye it? And…how many times has the Tooth Fairy visited?" She shook her head, frowning slightly. "After all she's been through, she sure doesn't need a bunch of doctor appointments while she's trying to settle in here at home." Rena paused, as if to catch her breath. "And what about us? What does she remember of *us*?"

This one, Grant could answer. At least in part. "She was told that we were killed in a drunk-driving accident," he said. "And that we'd named this…that nut job as Rosie's guardian. Unless something is seriously wrong—and I doubt it, since Agent Gonzalez didn't pass that info along to Detective Campbell—we'll take her to see a specialist. After she's had some time to adjust, I mean."

Rena wouldn't have to wonder about any of this if she'd been paying attention during the field trip.

Fair or not, it was how he felt. How he'd felt since she'd called the office that day, crying so hard he could barely understand a word she said. But they had to at least try to get along, for Rosie's sake. Grant knew he'd better keep his lips zipped.

"You probably won't believe this," she said, "given some of the, ah, discussions we had before I left, but…"

Discussions. He nearly chuckled. They'd had bitter quarrels. Full-blown shouting matches. Well, *he'd* shouted. A lot. Told Rena she was responsible for what happened to Rosie.

"…but I always held on to a thread of hope that someday, *someday*, she'd be found. I know it goes against everything I said back then, because I was trying so hard to accept things, to adjust and adapt, for both of our sakes, but I can't tell you what a relief it is, knowing she's coming home."

She'd held on to a *thread* of hope? It was all Grant could do to keep from groaning. Rena had been way too eager to pack up all their girl's things and stow them in the attic, beside his dusty childhood toys, her grandpa's steamer trunk and her grandmother's hope chest—the one that still housed Rena's wedding dress—his dad's tattered college textbooks, and Christmas decorations. Out of sight, out of mind, apparently. How could she feel that way about their sweet Rosie?

Plus, how many times had she accused him of living in the past, of refusing to accept that Rosie was gone? And all this time, she'd clung to hope, too? A hope, she'd told him often, that was impossible.

And then there was the way she'd pestered him to have another kid…and how he'd accused *her* of being cold, indifferent, heartless to think the birth of another child could blot out the agony they'd suffered. Rosie couldn't be replaced that easily. Why hadn't he been able to make her see that?

Grant put down his fork. He'd been famished when he sat down. Now, his appetite was gone. He started to push back from the table.

"Oh, don't leave yet," Rena said, a note of pleading in her voice. "I made dessert."

"I'm really not hungry, Rena."

He hadn't intended for the comment to sound harsh. But what did she expect? They hadn't shared a meal—or anything else—in *years*! Surely Rena didn't they'd simply pick up where they'd left off.

"Not even for chocolate pie?"

His favorite dessert. She'd only had an hour to throw dinner together, so she must have bought it when she'd stopped at the Giant for groceries. What the heck. Maybe something sweet would turn his sour mood around…

"Okay, but just a small slice."

"Whipped cream on top? I made plenty when I was beating up the filling."

So she'd *made* the pie, just for him? He marveled that she'd had time.

"Sure. Why not."

Rena got up and cleared their plates, and quickly replaced them with dessert.

"There's coffee—decaf—if you'd like some," she said.

"Well, since it's already made, no sense wasting it."

She poured them each a cup. Placed the sugar bowl and creamer near his elbow.

So. His favorite meal. His favorite dessert. And she'd remembered exactly how he liked his coffee. He could accuse her of trying to

soften him up. But for *what*? They were supposed to put on a united front, right? How
could they accomplish that without courtesy
and the occasional nicety?

He felt a pang of guilt. Had she really believed Rosie had been murdered? If so, she'd
suffered those thoughts alone. Even if she
hadn't left, Rena couldn't have talked to him
about it. He could barely stand to look at her
let alone talk about the kidnapping. She'd
made the right move, leaving when she did,
because if she'd stayed, their relationship
would only have deteriorated further. He'd
drawn some comfort from missing her now
and then, even though it made him feel a
little crazy. Because no rational man could
love and miss his wife…and deeply resent
her, all at the same time.

"Pie's good," he said, mostly to fill the
brittle silence.

"I'm glad you like it. I wasn't sure I remembered how to make it."

"You like it, too. You never made it for
your…guests?"

Man, talk about being obvious. If he

wanted to know if she was seeing someone, why not just ask?

Because he didn't want to picture her in
the arms of another man. She was still his
wife, after all.

"I didn't have much company. My cottage
is tiny. Barely enough space for a table for
two. And my life there is mostly work and
the occasional visit from Lilly, my landlady,
who lives in the big house next door. She's
a retired school bus driver. Trust me, I don't
invite a lot of interaction with her, lovely as
she is. Being around her, listening to her talk
about her tiny passengers only reminds me
of…" She looked away.

He'd avoided people—and places and
things—that reminded him of Rosie, too.
Even kept her bedroom door shut most of the
time, so he wouldn't have to look at her toys
and games, or the bed where he'd cuddled
with her while reading bedtime stories. How
much easier would everything have been if
they'd found a way to hold each other up
when the memories got tough to bear?

Water under the bridge, he thought. Deep,
dark, murky water…

"Want some help with these dishes?" he offered.

"No, but thanks. I'll have this cleaned up in no time. And then I'll get busy in the bedroom, so if you need to get in there before we leave for the airport—"

"Don't rush on my account. The Orioles are playing Detroit." He grabbed a bottle of water from the fridge. "Holler if you need anything."

He'd given it a lot of thought. Rosie would have more than enough to adjust to without seeing him and Rena in separate bedrooms. But how would he introduce the subject of her moving back into the master? And how in God's name was he going to share his bed with her again when he could barely tolerate sitting across the table from her?

Better figure it out, and fast, he told himself. Because tomorrow night, or the next, that was exactly what he'd have to do.

Or did he?

SEVERAL TIMES AS Rena moved her belongings into the master bedroom, she and Grant passed each another in the hall. He'd stuttered and stammered while explaining that, although he'd made up the guest bed for her, he hoped she'd give serious consideration to moving into their old room with him. For Rosie's sake. Every muscle in her had tensed, every nerve end jangled, yet she'd heard herself say "We can give it a try, I suppose." Now, the way he scooted along the wall to avoid brushing up against her left Rena wondering how he'd get any sleep, sharing the same bed.

She'd play it by ear; if he seemed fitful and agitated, Rena could always sleep on the family room sofa, and explain any questions from Rosie by claiming to have fallen asleep reading or watching TV.

It was the least she could do for him, after all she'd put him through.

Rena tidied the guest room, the kitchen and the master bedroom—though there wasn't much to do—mostly to stay out of his way until they had to leave for the airport.

Finally, it was time to head to BWI. At the start of the drive, Rena tested topics of conversation that wouldn't add to the tension between them. Unfortunately, the sound of her voice seemed enough to stress Grant further. She could tell by the way he gripped the steering wheel and stared straight ahead. It was what he'd done years ago in traffic jams, or if he made a wrong turn. Fortunately, she'd packed magazines and her e-reader along with his stack of important papers. At least she could pretend to have something to focus on during the three-hour flight besides his angry, stony silence.

Martha had posed a difficult question during their last session: "What will you do if Grant never forgives you?" Her answer had inspired the therapist's disapproving frown. "Why should I expect him to forgive me when I'll never forgive *myself*?"

Perhaps in time, they'd at least come to a meeting of the minds, find a certain peace with the living arrangements. But she wouldn't drive herself mad hoping things would eventually go back to where they'd been before, when he'd been a chatty, friendly, fun and funny partner. Far better and healthier to simply accept the status quo. *Besides, you'll have plenty to do, helping Rosie readjust.*

"What kind of car do you think we should rent?"

The suddenness of his voice startled her, and she masked it by toying with the hem of her jacket.

"I'm not sure, but we should ask if they rent children's booster seats."

He didn't respond at first. "I hadn't even given that a thought. But we'll have to turn it in with the car. What'll we do on the drive home from BWI?"

"It's only twenty minutes. You'll stay in the slow lane the whole way, and I'll ride in the back with Rosie." She chanced a peek at his stern profile. "Not that I think anything will happen—you've always been a good, safe driver. But on the off chance it does, I can protect her."

He gave a tiny grunt. Rena braced herself for him to say, *"The way you protected her years ago?"*

"That'll work, I guess," he said instead, and Rena sighed in relief. "We can't very well take her into a big box store and buy one."

"Why not?"

"She'll be overwhelmed, that's why. Seeing that woman, lying dead on the mall
floor. Being carted off by the cops, then in-
terrogated by one shrink after another, then
shuttled to a foster home. It's too much."

For Rosie, or for him? she wondered.

"We will need to take her shopping eventually, anyway. It isn't likely she'll have
much to wear. We can pick up a few of
the essentials, along with the car seat. You
know, shoes. Underwear and socks. Pajamas
and slippers. And the weather can get chilly
in May." Rena paused. Was he even listening? "She'll need a jacket, too."

He continued staring straight ahead,
gripping the steering wheel so tightly that
his knuckles turned white. Was she strong
enough to endure his loathing for…for who
knew how long? She'd have to be, because
Rosie should *not* be exposed to conflict of
any kind. Rena didn't need to think for very
long to come up with examples of their little
girl's reaction to discord between her parents…

One snowy day, when Grant forgot that it
was his turn to pick Rosie up at preschool,

Rena had been forced to leave the hospital early, which hadn't gone over well with the head nurse. Over supper that night, she'd pointed out that she'd grown tired of being called on the carpet by her boss every time a meeting took precedence over his duties as a father. "My boss," Rena had told him, "made it clear that there are plenty of experienced nurses on the roster who can work a full, uninterrupted day." Grant's angry retort? He'd had clients, important clients, whose fees helped pay for day care, weekend trips to Ocean City, Christmas gifts and more. Rosie's worried expression had stopped Rena from pointing out that *her* salary contributed to the family coffers, too.

And then there was the time when he'd promised to leave work early to take Rosie to her well visit at the pediatrician's. A full-of-questions client and an accident on the Beltway, he'd all but shouted, were to blame. Not his forgetfulness. It wasn't until he'd noticed Rosie's teary eyes that he softened his tone and offered a half-hearted apology.

Stop dwelling on the negatives; there are plenty of good things about Grant...

His love of family gatherings, for one thing. And he'd never admit it, but Grant enjoyed chick flicks almost as much as she did. And what about his fondness for puns? When she brought home a copy of *How Weather Works* to read with Rosie, he sat down beside them and said, "I'm reading a book about anti-gravity. It's impossible to put down." And while replacing the door-knocker on the front door, he'd said, "Bet you didn't know that the guy who invented this contraption got a no-bell prize…"

The memories should have lifted her spirits. Instead, they woke a deep sadness. Rena hung her head. In the blink of an eye—literally—she'd lost their only child, and the man Grant used to be.

She'd missed him. Missed him during those many difficult months after Rosie was taken. Missed him every day that she'd been gone. Missed him now, even though he was arm's length away.

"Why so quiet?" he wanted to know.

Rena exhaled. "Just thinking."

"Yeah, it's a lot to take in."

Reaching across the console, he patted her

hands, clasped tightly in her lap. "Stop worrying, Rena. We'll get through it. We have to. Rosie's counting on us."

In other words, he'd make the ultimate sacrifice and put up with *her*...for Rosie's sake. Oh, how she wished she knew how to make amends so he could see his way clear to forgiving her. How she wished she could get that life-changing moment back...

He maneuvered the car into a space at the airport's Quick Park, and before she managed to gather her enormous purse and jacket, he'd opened the passenger door. In her hurry to exit the vehicle, she dropped the bag, spilling the contents onto the blacktop.

Squatting, she grabbed a ballpoint, a tube of lipstick, her compact. "Sorry," she said, stuffing them back into the bag. "I need to remember to zip this stupid thing."

What was truly stupid, she thought, were the tears that filled her eyes, just as they had in Rosie's room. And, as he'd done earlier, Grant took a knee and helped her clean up the mess. He got to his feet and held out a hand. Rena hesitated, then let him help her up. His fingers, strong and warm, wrapped around hers, and for a moment, there under the streetlamp, he looked at her, as if seeing her for the first time since she'd left for Fenwick Island.

"You look bone-tired," he said, shoving the envelope into her bag.

"Wow. Aren't you good for a girl's ego."

One corner of his mouth lifted with the hint of a smile. "Didn't mean it that way. You're gorgeous, as always. Just..." His lips formed a taut line as he zipped the bag. "Maybe you can grab a quick nap during our flight."

In all their months apart, she'd barely slept more than four hours a night. A nap, seated beside him on a crowded plane? Impossible. But as the airport shuttle rolled to a stop behind his car, Rena said, "Maybe."

Grant slid their suitcases into the luggage rack, then took her elbow and guided her to the only empty seats, all the way in the back of the bus. Last time he'd done such a thing had been when they took Rosie to Disney World weeks before the abduction. Once they'd settled into their seats, he'd pulled Rosie into his lap and, grinning, pressed a kiss to her cheek. Pressed one to Rena's, too. "Mickey Mouse, here we come!" Judging by the excitement in his voice and the delighted glint in his eyes, one might have thought the trip was for him, not their daughter.

A car pulled out in front of the shuttle, forcing the driver to slam on the brakes... and causing Rena to lose her balance. If Grant hadn't wrapped a protective arm around her, she'd have ended up on the gritty black floor.

"Idiot," the driver muttered, then quickly added, "Everybody okay?"

As a chorus of yeses filled the shuttle, Grant continued to hold her. It felt good. Felt *right*. In a perfect world, she could pretend his reaction meant he still cared for her. But their world hadn't been perfect in years.

"Thanks. You saved me from skinned knees, or worse."

Leaning back, he withdrew his arm. "No problem. I would have done it for anyone."

Yes, he would. Rena's heart ached a little that he'd felt it necessary to point that out.

"We'll have some time to kill once we get

to the gate," he said. "Think I'll call Mom, bring her up to speed on…everything."

"Good idea. I know how she worries." Rena looked toward the shuttle's windshield and added, "How much does she know?"

"Pretty much what we do. That Rosie is in Chicago, and we're going to bring her home."

"Southwest," the driver called, rising to help Grant with the suitcases. "Have a safe flight," he said, pocketing the bills Grant had pressed into his hand.

Gripping both suitcase handles, Grant led the way into the terminal.

"Here y'go," he said, handing her the printout of her boarding pass.

She thanked him. "Let me know how much I owe you."

His eyebrows drew together and his lips formed a thin line. "For Pete's sake, Rena, You don't owe me anything. You're still my wife, like it or not."

In her mind, she'd always be his wife, even if he filed for divorce.

Side by side, they moved a step closer to the check-in kiosk.

"I just didn't want to start out on the wrong foot," she explained.

"You're not." His expression softened slightly. "I'm glad you're here. Don't know how I'd get through this alone."

It was the first kind thing he'd said to her in years. *Don't get all moony-eyed. It doesn't mean there's hope for a real reconciliation.*

He took her boarding pass, and as he poked at the choices on the screen, she thought: *It doesn't mean there isn't, either.*

CHAPTER FIVE

"Plane takes off in about an hour," Grant said into the phone. "Just wanted you to know we're on our way."

"How does Rena look?" his mom asked. "I talk to her fairly often, but I haven't seen her since the day she left."

"She looks good." He risked a glance over his shoulder to where she sat, flipping through one of the magazines she'd packed. Even from twenty feet away, he could see those long lashes, dusting her freckled cheeks.

"You're being nice, I hope."

"Mom. Come on. 'Course I am." *Nice as I can be, anyway, under the circumstances.*

"Good. Because whether you admit it or not, what happened isn't her fault. If I had a dollar for every time you got away from me when you were a boy—"

"You could buy us an order of French fries."

Tina's sigh filtered into his ear. Almost from the day he'd introduced them, his mom had thought of Rena as a daughter. Her moving to Fenwick Island hadn't changed that. If anything, their bond had deepened, thanks to twice-weekly phone calls.

"Just promise me you'll set aside your hatred and focus on all the good times you two shared before—"

"Mom, I don't hate her!" he said, a tad louder than intended. Lowering his voice, he continued. "We're getting along fine. I'm doing everything in my power to be civil."

"Civil." Tina sighed again. "That's not good enough, Grant. She deserves better, and you know it."

Okay, so Rena had been a good wife, and for the most part, a good mom, too. *Not good enough to prevent the kidnapping, but...*

"They'll make the all-aboard announcement soon, and I want to find some coffee and something for us to eat during the flight."

"Good idea. Get tuna. Rena loves tuna."

He didn't tell her that Rena hated the stuff, that she'd only pretended to like his mom's recipe to spare her feelings.

"Call you soon as I know more."

"Tell Rena I send my love."

"I will," he said, hanging up as he closed the space between him and Rena.

Using her thumb, she marked her page in the magazine. "How's your mom?"

"She's good. Excited to see Rosie. Told me to give you her love."

Nodding, Rena smiled. Not enough to light up those amazing green eyes, but it sure beat the unhappiness that had been there before.

"How 'bout you stay with the bags while I scrounge up something for us to eat. Those puny bags of peanuts they serve on the plane won't tide us over until breakfast." He grinned. "Mom suggested tuna for you…"

Rena wrinkled her nose. "I'd rather make do with the peanuts."

He pointed. "There's a sandwich shop. You okay with a cheeseburgers and fries?"

"Sure. That'll work."

"What do you want to drink?"

"Surprise me."

She looked so vulnerable in the harsh glare of the overhead lights. It made him want to sit down, wrap her in a comforting hug and remind her what he'd said earlier... that everything would be all right. Because the truth was, he needed the reassurance, too.

Ten minutes later, as they buckled up on the plane, their fingers touched. Hers were cold and trembly, but he resisted the urge to warm them between his own.

"Tell me again what Agent Gonzalez said about Rosie's checkup?"

She'd crossed both arms over her chest, freeing the armrest for him. Why did she have to be so thoughtful? Didn't she realize how tough she was making it to stay mad at her?

Grant took a deep breath, summoning patience. "He said she's fine, physically. Not a scratch on her. And no evidence at all of..." He couldn't bring himself to say it. "...you know."

She exhaled a shaky sigh.

"The psychologist said it's too soon to

tell if there's any emotional damage." He shrugged one shoulder. "But since Rosie wouldn't talk much about this *Barbara* person…"

"I liked it better when she didn't have a name. It made it easier to hate her."

It seemed to Grant that Rena was thinking out loud, so he continued with the information Gonzalez had provided: after interviewing Barbara Smith's family and friends, the police had discovered that she'd lost her own child, a girl, when a drunk driver barreled into her car, head-on. According to her sister, Barbara had nearly lost her mind, and isolated herself from her extended family. They'd heard through one of her neighbors that she'd adopted a child—referred to only as Ruby—but the rift had remained. Since Barbara had stubbornly continued to reject attempts at reconciliation, the family had never met the child. If not for the aneurism, Grant and Rena would likely never have seen Rosie again.

"I hope the foster family is nice. She's already been through so much."

Grant only nodded. This wasn't the time

or place to point out that if not for her negligence…

"Did the agent know what this…this *woman* told Rosie? To keep her from calling attention to herself, I mean?"

"She told her that you two went to college together, that you were the best of friends, that we'd asked her to be Rosie's guardian in case something happened to us."

Rena gasped. "No…"

He shook his head. "'Fraid so. She told Rosie we were killed in a horrible accident on I-95, and since she was named in our will as the legal guardian…"

"And Rosie believed her. Oh, the poor little thing!" She hid her face behind her hands. "How did she explain that I was right there beside her at that field trip, not in a car on the interstate?"

"She wasn't old enough to question it."

"But she asked questions. I'm sure of it. *Lots* of questions. Remember how we used to laugh at how she could turn any situation, no matter how mundane, into a Q and A session?"

Yes, he remembered, and the image of her

upturned, animated little face, eyes wide as she peppered them with things like "Why do dogs' claws stick out but cats' don't?" and "How does the sun know when it's morning?" nearly brought tears to his eyes.

Rena turned slightly in her seat and looked into his eyes. "Did the agent say anything about photographs? Maybe I'll recognize Barbara. Maybe—"

"Even if you did, there's not much we could do with the information now."

Shoulders drooping, she sat back.

"Let's keep a good thought, okay? Focus on the fact that Gonzalez said Rosie left him with the impression that she's a well-adjusted kid."

"That's ridiculous. She learned to do and say whatever that crazy woman wanted." Fingertips pressed to her temples, Rena groaned quietly. "And isn't it the irony of ironies that, in her little-girl mind, she lost both of her parents *and* her…and this *Barbara* person in the span of a few years!" She pounded a fist on the armrest. "It's a good thing she's dead because I swear, I'd strangle her."

"Yeah, well, you'd have to get in line behind me."

The man in the window seat cleared his throat. Loudly. No doubt the whole thing sounded like a TV crime drama to him.

Grant and Rena exchanged an *oops* look, and for a moment or two, sat silently, staring at their tray tables.

"Small consolation, I know," he whispered, "but they have a child psychiatrist—or psychologist, I forget what type Dr. Robson is—on stand-by. I'm sure she'll explain everything."

"And have plenty of suggestions about how we'll need to, for lack of a better word, handle Rosie once we get her home."

"Well, small consolation at this point, but Gonzalez said he had a good feeling about this case."

Eyes closed, Rena leaned her head against the seatback. "You know the old saying…"

Grant thought he knew what she'd say. "'From his lips to God's ears'?"

"Exactly," she agreed, her voice a barely audible whisper.

Something his mom had said a few weeks

ago came to mind. *"You're not the only one who's suffering, you know. Rena has been torturing herself with guilt."*

That's how I'd feel if I'd put some other kid's welfare ahead of Rosie's.

Grant ground his molars together. Thoughts like that could only make matters worse. The coming weeks and months would be tough enough; reverting to his former surly behavior would make things unbearable.

"LEE HAS RESCHEDULED all my client meetings," Grant said as he steered their grey rental sedan out of the airport lot. "I told her, 'indefinitely.'"

"And I cleared things with my boss. She assured me I'll still have a job…if I come back."

If? Grant shrugged. They hadn't exactly had a chance to discuss the long-term. He already knew guarding his heart wouldn't be easy once they started living as man and wife again. How long could he keep it up?

Rena sat quietly, staring out the passenger window for several minutes, then said,

"I know you're still angry with me. I don't blame you because I'm still angry with myself, and I realize I don't deserve your understanding and kindness and…whatever, so I really appreciate the way you've been treating me."

How was he supposed to react to that?

"In a quarter mile," said the British voice of the GPS, "turn right."

Grant maneuvered onto the off-ramp. So far, he'd done a fair-to-middlin' job of keeping his feelings in check, but he just wasn't ready to go there with Rena tonight. Maybe he'd never be ready to get close to her again. In that case, they'd have to find a way to help Rosie understand that they'd always be there, together, for her—even if their marriage ended.

Grant shook his head. How would he explain it to his little girl when he didn't understand it himself?

The separation had unofficially begun a full year before Rena left for Fenwick Island. It had been her idea to move into the guest room, and while something had told him that if they hoped to salvage what was left of their marriage, he ought to discourage it, he'd let her go. When she suggested moving to Fenwick Island, he'd let her go yet again. Funny thing was, they'd been apart nearly eight months before he'd stopped reaching for her first thing in the morning, to stroke her soft hair, touch her shoulder, run a fingertip down her cheek. Would the old, loving habit resurface once she moved back into their room? In his opinion, she looked her prettiest right after she woke up, with tousled hair and a makeup-free face.

Suddenly, he felt sorry for her—a surprise, since for so long he'd felt little more than bitterness. On the phone earlier, Grant's mom had made him promise to treat Rena with kindness, as much for his and Rosie's sake as Rena's. He'd meant it when he said he didn't hate her. Oh, he'd tried, but memories of her lyrical voice and the sweetness of her temperament smothered the emotion, just as surely as water douses a fire.

Unfortunately, none of that changed the fact that her carelessness cost him his daughter.

"Are you all right?"

Her voice startled him, and he said, "I'm fine." He looked over at her. "Why?"

"You've barely said a word since we hit the road."

"Just...just a lot on my mind."

"Yeah, it's pretty daunting, isn't it?"

She could say that again.

"If I could spare you all of this..."

Should have thought of that during the field trip.

But that was no way to start things. Not if he hoped to do what was best for Rosie.

"Look. Rena. We're gonna get through this. We have to—"

"—for Rosie's sake," they said together.

One hundred percent truth, he thought. Rosie had been an astute, sensitive child. Even the tiniest spat between him and Rena had the power to put tears in her eyes. Seeing their daughter upset had been all it took to inspire an apology from Rena, even if he'd clearly been in the wrong. Keeping the peace at any cost must have been programmed into her DNA.

Had that changed? Or would Rena still be willing to pay any price to protect Rosie?

If she'd held that mindset that day at the zoo…

CHAPTER SIX

ONCE THE NECESSARY interviews and paperwork were complete, Agent Gonzalez handed Grant directions to the psychiatrist's office. He took note of Rena's thin smile. It was what she'd always done when trying to hide displeasure. Wasn't his fault, was it, that the guy was more comfortable with him than Rena. She could just as easily have stayed in touch with the agent.

"Dr. Robson is better equipped to take care of a kid," he said, walking them toward the building's entrance, "so I suggested that she take your little girl over there. Who knows what sort of madness Rosie would see or hear if she hung around the station much longer."

"We appreciate that," Grant said, shaking the man's hand.

"And we appreciate your patience and understanding," Rena said. "We pretty much bombarded you with questions."

"Happy to be of service." The agent handed her a business card. "If you have any more questions, call me. Any time." He grinned. "Can't promise I'll be much help, but I'll do my level best. I'll give Detective Campbell a call, get him caught up. He'll probably want to talk with both of you once you're settled in, you know, to dot any i's and cross any t's we might have missed."

Grant pressed a palm to Rena's lower back and guided her toward the parking lot.

"What time is your flight tomorrow?" Gonzalez asked.

"Noon. But we can change it if we need to."

"Don't worry. Dr. Robson is the best at what she does. She'll have you out of there in plenty of time to grab a bite to eat and catch a few z's tonight. Be sure to give yourself plenty of time in the morning, though. O'Hare is a zoo."

When they reached the psychiatrist's office, the woman at the reception desk smiled. "May I help you?"

"We're the VanMeters," Grant said, "here for our—"

"Yes, of course. The doctor is just wrapping up a session. May I get you anything while you wait? Coffee? Tea? Soda?"

"Water if you have it," Rena said. "I'm dry as the Sahara."

The woman reached into a small fridge behind the counter and withdrew two bright blue bottles. "There you go. Make yourselves comfortable. I'm sure Dr. Robson will be with you shortly."

Grant and Rena sat stiff and quiet on the sofa nearest the reception counter. Seeing that Rena was having trouble opening the bottle, he took it from her and unscrewed the cap.

"Thanks," she said when he handed it back. "And please don't tell me I don't need to say thank-you. It's a habit. Ungrateful people quickly wear out their welcome, and that's the last thing I want to do. Especially now."

Her knee was bouncing out a quick rhythm. She was obviously feeling as keyed up as he was.

"Okay," he began, "from now on I—"

The door beside the reception desk opened. A gaunt, bearded man exited the office, and close on his heels, a scowling boy of twelve or thirteen. Behind them, a middle-aged redhead said, "See you next week, all right?"

The man nodded and the boy said something unintelligible as they left.

"You must be the VanMeters," the doctor said. She took a few steps closer and extended her right hand. "I'm Dr. Robson. Please, come right in."

They sat in the overstuffed leather chairs facing her desk.

"I see Marcie got you something to drink." She plopped onto the seat of a high-backed swivel chair and proceeded to page through a file. "Need anything else before we begin?"

"Thanks," Grant said, "but we'd rather just get on with things."

His abrupt tone caused the doctor's right eyebrow to lift slightly. To soften the blow, Rena tacked on, "So we can see Rosie as soon as possible."

"It's been my experience that situations like these are extremely traumatizing for families. I understand you two are separated?"

"I don't recall either of us mentioning that," Rena said.

"Agent Gonzalez prepares me well for dealing with children like Rosie."

"We've been living apart for a while," Grant told her, "but we haven't made the separation official."

She nodded. "Well, what's significant is that you've decided to partner up again for your daughter's sake. I'm sure you realize the importance of setting aside whatever differences you might still have, at least until we get an accurate read on how Rosie is coping with everything. I found her to be a bright, perceptive child."

Her way of reminding them that their little girl would sniff out a phony relationship in a heartbeat?

Dr. Robson patted the file. "Do you mind talking about the reasons for your separation?"

Rena looked to Grant, mostly to get a read on how he preferred to proceed, but he stared straight ahead.

"Grant didn't ask me to leave, if that's what you're getting at."

The doctor remained silent. Waiting, watching.

"I guess if I boiled it down to one thing, guilt was the major motivator in my decision. My attitude and behavior spilled into our everyday lives and made us both pretty miserable."

Robson focused on Grant. "Is that how you see things, too?"

He shrugged one shoulder. "Sometimes," he said, drawing out the word. "Guilt and blame go hand in hand. I wasn't exactly easy to live with, either."

"Is that your way of saying you blamed Rena for the kidnapping?"

Another shrug.

"You realize, of course," Robson continued, "that what happened could have happened to anyone, even the most diligent parent."

Knowing Grant, he probably felt a little

like a butterfly, pinned to a mat. Tina had come right out and admitted she'd told him the same thing, many times.

"It's the logical way to view the situation," Rena said. "But when it's *your* child, it's hard not to place blame. Nothing can change the fact that I looked away just long enough to enable the kidnapper. It's something I'll have to live with forever. Something I'll spend the rest of my days trying to atone for."

"Ah, so you were the only parent chaperone on the field trip?"

"Of course not. There were six, maybe seven moms in all, but they were all looking out for the children assigned to them. I can't—*won't*—blame anyone else."

"That's the trouble with self-importance," the doctor said slowly. "It tends to take a terrible toll on the individual." She paused then added, "For Rosie's sake, you need to find another way to deal with your feelings, Mrs. VanMeter."

Almost word for word what Martha had said. It hadn't helped then, and it wasn't helping now.

"If you insist on beating yourself up, you'll need to find a way to do it in private. Even then, there's a chance Rosie will pick up on it."

She turned her attention to Grant again. "And you'll need to set aside your anger toward Rena, at least in the presence of your daughter. I'm happy to recommend a marriage counselor that you can see in addition to whomever you choose for Rosie." She raised an eyebrow. "Unless neither of you believes a reconciliation is possible."

Why had Robson aimed the question at her, instead of Grant? *Maybe,* Rena thought, *because she thinks you'll give a more straightforward answer...*

"I can't speak for Grant, but I'm certainly not opposed to getting back together. Permanently." She could feel his eyes on her. Hopefully, her response hadn't riled him further.

"Grant?" Robson said. "Do you feel the same way?"

"I, ah, well, I guess I'm not totally opposed to it."

"Do I detect a *but* in your answer?"

He sat up straighter and crossed his arms over his chest. "Look. Doctor. You said what's really important is that we set aside our differences, especially in Rosie's presence. And I agree with that. Is it possible we'll resolve the marriage problems while we're faking it?" Yet another shrug. "Who knows? All I can say for sure is that I'll do anything, *anything* to help my girl."

How had he managed to sound surly and nonchalant at the same time? Rena wondered. *Faking it.* He could have slapped her and it wouldn't have hurt as much.

Robson turned to another page in the file. "Will you be returning to work, Rena?"

In her opinion, this felt a lot more like an interrogation than a meeting to discuss what was best for Rosie. From the sound of things, Dr. Robson was looking for reasons *not* to send Rosie home with them.

She chose her words carefully. "No. For the time being, anyway, I have no plans to look for a new job. I want to be available twenty-four seven until I'm sure Rosie is all right, that she has acclimated to all of us being together again. And just so you know, Grant is taking some time off work, too." She crossed her legs, and tugged at the hem of her skirt. "Agent Gonzalez told us he gave you a letter, written by the kidnapper? That there are things in it Grant and I need to hear?"

"Yes, that's true. But let's not rush."

"Rosie and Rena and I have been apart long enough," Grant ground out. "I say we cut to the chase, do whatever needs doing to put us together with her, ASAP."

The doctor walked around to the front of her desk and sat on its corner, tapping an envelope against a heavy wooden nameplate.

"Oh, my," Rena said. "My hands are shaking so badly, the words will blur."

"I'm happy to read it aloud, if you like," Robson said, "but if you'd rather, I'll give you a few minutes to read it in private."

Rena met Grant's eyes. "It's up to you."

"Go ahead," he told the doctor. "Read it. We'll read it again later. At the hotel."

She'd already stressed that they'd need to come back in the morning when, after Robson had a chance to observe the threesome and share her expert opinion on how to proceed, they could begin their trip home. Last night, they'd struggled to find things to talk about, and while lovely, the room hadn't provided a place to escape from awkward silences. At least tonight, they'd have Barbara's letter to discuss.

The doctor returned to her chair and swiveled to face them, head on.

"As you'll recall," Robson said, "Ms. Smith left this letter with her sister, with instructions that it was to be delivered *unopened* to the authorities in the event of her demise." She slid the pages from the envelope. "Agent Gonzalez has a copy in his file, as do I. This is the original, and it's for you.

"I've spoken with the sister—and several other close relatives—about this matter. They were horrified to learn what Barbara had done, but they'd never met Rosie—or Ruby, as Barbara called her."

"How many relatives were there?"

"Just the sister and her grown children. They lived relatively nearby."

"But they never met her?"

"According to my interviews, they did not."

"Good. Because…I can't speak for Grant, but I'm not in favor of visiting rights!"

Rena might as well have remained silent for all the attention the doctor paid her comment.

"Her sister told me that Barbara was suicidal after losing her husband and child. Sounds like she suffered survivor's guilt."

"Agent Gonzalez told me the drunk driver only got five years? That must have made things tougher," Grant said.

Robson sniffed. "The man had a good lawyer, for one thing, and it was his first offense, for another. Throw in a sympathetic judge…" She ran a hand across the tidy handwriting that filled the first page of the letter. "I think learning more about her will make it easier for you to understand what she did."

"Understand? You must be joking!" Rena said. "Nothing you say, and nothing in that letter can make me understand how a person steals someone else's child. Grant and I lived without Rosie for *years* because of her. She took a part of us when she took Rosie. Losing her nearly destroyed us, but we didn't go out and kidnap someone else's child to ease our pain!"

Rena felt the heat of an angry blush coloring her cheeks. The office grew quiet, so quiet she could hear the steady swish of the pendulum, swaying right and left in the body of Robson's stately grandfather clock. What was the woman waiting for…her or Grant to say that they'd split up because it seemed less agonizing than holding on to one another?

"While I agree with Rena, we're not any closer to seeing Rosie, now are we?" Grant pointed out.

"I just want to take a moment to stress how important it is that you're honest with yourselves. If you aren't absolutely sure you can present a united front, it'll be better for Rosie if you sit her down and tell her the truth about your relationship, right away."

Rena imagined the scene… Rosie, teary-eyed and frightened by the prospect of being shuttled from Grant's house to hers. "Dr. Robson—"

"Fiona, please."

After tomorrow, they'd never see her

again, so Rena saw no reason to feign a friendly relationship. Except that the doctor might see her reluctance to agree as a character trait that might be damaging to Rosie. She decided to play nice.

"We've barely had a chance to adjust to the situation, ourselves. There hasn't been time to discuss exactly how we'll make it work. But I can assure you of one thing. We. *Will*. Make. It. Work."

Robson returned to her chair. "Good. I'm relieved to hear that. Because from what I gathered through interviews with Rosie and studying her behavior, she's handling things admirably. It's possible she'll adapt quickly and easily to being with you, to being home again." She raised an eyebrow. "That said, she will most likely have some issues related to Barbara's death. She told Rosie you two were gone, then stepped into your shoes. Now that Rosie knows you're alive and well, and that Barbara lied to her... Well, all that is bound to cause a few problems.

"Don't be overly concerned, though. As I said, she seems like a well-adjusted little girl, despite all she's been through. So, much as I hate to repeat myself, if you can't pull off the whole together again thing, tell her. Tell her now. She won't be happy, but she'll adapt. She's a resilient kid."

"Tell her?" Grant all but shouted. "Out of the question! She's just a little girl! A little girl who's been through more these past few years than most adults go through in a lifetime. Life has made too many demands on her already. Dealing with the breakup of her parents..." He ran a hand through his hair. "It's not going to happen. She needs to know she can count on us." He glanced over at Rena. "We're in this for the long haul, right?"

Rena searched his face and saw how much he needed her to say yes. And so she did.

Facing Robson, she said, "We're not so naïve that we think it'll be a cakewalk, but we have the best incentive in the world to make the marriage work—*Rosie*."

It did her heart good to hear Grant's relieved sigh.

"You know," Robson said, "I agree with Manuel. I think you guys are going to do fine, just fine."

With that, she put on her glasses and picked up the letter. Rena didn't know what possessed her to do it, but she reached for Grant's hand. He took it, gave it a slight squeeze, and held it against his chest.

"'To whom it may concern,'" Robson began. "'In the event of my death, it should be known that Ruby Smith is not my daughter. Her real name is Rosie, and she belongs to Grant and Rena VanMeter, who live in Ellicott City, a suburb of Baltimore, Maryland.'"

The letter went on to explain how she'd been in town visiting a friend in the hope that a few months away from Chicago would help her put the loss behind her, once and for all. During a trip to the Columbia Mall, she'd noticed Rosie on the ornate carousel as her mother watched from a few feet away. She'd struck up a conversation with the mother, asking which child was hers.

And then Rena remembered... If the woman hadn't spoken to her, she might not have noticed her at all. And if not for her unhappy eyes and wavering voice, Rena probably would have pretended not to hear the question. "That one," she'd said. "That's my Rosie. And yours?" As the ride slowed, the woman pointed, too, at a brown-haired boy in one of the booth seats. Rena had moved toward the gate, saying "Aw, he's cute," and immediately turned her attention to Rosie, who'd skipped up to remind her about getting ice cream afterward.

It hadn't been the only time Rena had seen the woman. At the pet store a few weeks later, she saw her again, standing alone as Rosie and a few other children played with a litter of kittens. Correction, Rena realized, she'd been watching *Rosie*. Was it possible that if she'd found a way to speak to Barbara that day…or if she'd spotted her weeks later, at the petting zoo, she might have prevented the kidnapping?

Agent Gonzalez could shed light on that, and tomorrow, she'd present him with the information. Right now, Rena only wanted to get the whole letter-reading ordeal over with, because the sooner that was behind them, the sooner they'd see their precious child.

"'I know how hard it must have been for her parents, but I won't say I'm sorry,'"

Robson continued, "'because Ruby gave me years' worth of joy. If I had it all to do over again, I'd do it in a heartbeat. I want to assure them that I treated her well. She had everything she needed and then some.'" The doctor folded the letter and returned it to the envelope. "She signed it Barbara Smith," she said, handing it to Grant.

His hand was shaking as he leaned forward to accept it, sliding it into his shirt pocket without letting go of Rena's hand. "Is there anything else?"

The doctor got to her feet and plucked a business card from the holder on her desk. "No, we've covered everything, I believe." She gave the card to Grant, and this time he did let go of Rena.

"If you have any questions, feel free to call any time."

"Are we…are we going to see Rosie now?" Rena asked, following her to the door.

"We are. My advice? Do what feels natural. If hugs and kisses seem in order, give them."

"But…but how will we know?"

Robson stopped, laid a hand on Rena's

forearm and met her eyes. "From everything I've gathered from our little talk," she said, smiling, "I'm confident that you'll know." She paused. "Would you like to see pictures of her?"

"What I'd like," Rena said, "is to see my child."

The doctor nodded. "Okay, I'll go ahead and make sure everything is ready." She gestured toward a bench in the hall. "You guys have a seat."

Grant hesitated. "What do you mean, 'get everything ready'?"

"Rosie has been with my assistant, who's overseeing some artwork we asked her to do. Drawings provide us with a view into what's going on in kids' minds. They often say what they think we want to hear, but their pictures rarely lie."

Rena sat on the bench and Grant followed. "And if there's something disturbing in her pictures, then what?" he asked.

"Oh, don't worry. I don't expect to find anything out of the ordinary. Look at it this way. Even if there are signs of trouble, at least you'll have a heads-up—and so will the therapist you'll take her to at home. Fore-warned is forearmed, you know?"

"I suppose that makes sense," Rena said as Grant nodded.

"You suppose?"

"We haven't had time to talk to get a rec-ommendation from her pediatrician."

"No problem. I've compiled a list of spe-cialists in your area and put them into the envelope with Barbara's letter. They're all people with the skills and experience to deal with children like Rosie."

Children like Rosie, who'd been abducted and kept from their families for years…

"I'll come back for you in a few minutes."

The click-clack of her heels on the lino-leum ended when the door to 1420 closed behind her.

Eyes squeezed shut Grant looked at the ceiling. "Do me a favor, will ya?"

"Sure. Of course. Anything," she said, meaning it.

"If I start blubbering like a baby when I see her, whack me up-side the head."

"I won't need to. You're the strongest man

I've ever met. Not that crying would change that."

He scanned her face, as if searching for evidence that she'd meant it.

"Most stubborn, you mean."

What was he suggesting?

"I can't stand this," Rena burst out. "I want to see her. Right now."

Grant rested his elbows on his thighs and held his head in his hands. "I know. I hate waiting."

"I remember," she said. If he'd said it once, he'd said it a hundred times in their years together.

Grant clasped and unclasped his hands in the space between his knees. It's what he'd done in the ER when Rosie fell from the swing and broke her arm, and every other time he felt out of control.

She gave in to the urge to comfort him, and gave his shoulder a gentle squeeze. "A very wise man once told me not to worry, because everything would be all right."

Grant sat back. "Yeah, well..." He ran a hand through his hair. "Wonder what's taking so long?"

As if on cue, the door at the end of the hall opened and Robson leaned out. "We're ready for you."

"Are you as nervous as I am?" Grant whispered as they stood.

"My stomach is in knots. All I want to do is give her the biggest hug ever. I don't know if I'll be able to hold back."

"Maybe we won't have to make that decision. Maybe Rosie will hug *us*."

They stood just outside the heavy wooden door. Grant grasped the knob. "Ready?"

Rena squared her shoulders. "Ready as I'll ever be."

She followed him into a small waiting area between the entrance and another door. It was empty.

"Where did Robson disappear to?" Rena asked.

Grant didn't reply but simply crossed the room in three long strides and opened the door to the playroom. Rena took her place beside him.

And there she was.

Our Rosie.

Grant squatted down to her height. "Hey there, kiddo," he said.

Rosie looked at each of them in turn, and as her gaze settled on Grant's face, a slow smile lit up her face. "You look just like your picture. Just like I remembered."

Bending, Rena whispered, "Picture?"

"I emailed a couple photos of us," he whispered back. "In case Agent Gonzalez or Dr. Robson needed them for anything."

Rosie scrambled to her feet and, hands clasped at her waist, took a tentative step forward, and in that split-second, Rena wondered how much Rosie remembered from that day five years ago. Did she hate Rena for allowing another child's needs to distract her from her own little girl? How many times had Rosie thought about that moment? Was it the source of nightmares and day terrors? Had it scarred her forever?

Grant held out his arms, and Rosie ran to him. "Daddy, Daddy, oh, Daddy..."

Through her tears, Rena could see that Grant's eyes were moist, too.

"Ah, my sweet Rosie-girl," he said. For what seemed like a full five minutes, he held her tight and when he held her at arm's length, Rena saw that his tears had dampened the child's shoulder.

"Let me look at you." Bracketing her face with big, strong hands, he stared into her eyes. "You're a sight to behold, you know that? I'm so happy to see you!"

"I'm happy to see you, too!"

Rosie hadn't cast so much as a glance in Rena's direction.

And it broke her heart.

Rosie remembered. Did she hate her? Grant turned slightly, held out a hand to invite Rena closer. Kneeling beside him with arms extended, she waited, hoping her little girl would greet her as she'd greeted her dad.

"Go ahead, sweetie, give your mom a big hello hug."

Oh, how it hurt that she only moved closer because of Grant's gentle nudge! Rena wrapped her arms around her, willing herself to appreciate the momentary contact, to ignore the way Rosie stood, arms pressed tight to her sides, stiff as a statue.

Reminding herself it was only their first interaction, that Rosie had been through a lot and must be overwhelmed, Rena willed herself not to cry. Time, she decided, would heal any wounds her inattentiveness had caused her sweet daughter.

Time, and a major miracle…

Rena turned her loose, feigned a smile. Hands on the tiny shoulders, she said, "I missed you, sweet girl, missed you so much!"

The child's blank stare shook her to the core, threatening her tenuous hold on self-control. Clearly, Rosie didn't believe her. This was the stuff of nightmares.

Her only child hated her.

Rosie looked at Grant. "When are we going home?"

He straightened to his full height and Rosie grabbed his hand.

"Right now," he answered, his defiant expression a warning to the doctor that she'd best not disagree.

Robson, who'd been watching from a few yards away, said nothing.

Rosie read the woman's silence as rejection of Grant's straightforward statement.

"Does that mean I have to go back to the

Millers' house?" Rosie asked, her voice rising. "I don't want to sleep there again. Their house is a mess and those other kids are loud. And that *boy* pushes everybody!"

Robson frowned, and Rena didn't dare speak. One wrong word and the psychiatrist could decide to nix their plans.

Finally, Robson said, "We have a few more details to work out, papers to sign, things like that…"

"I don't mind waiting while you do those things," Rosie was quick to respond. "I'm really, really good at waiting. I'll sit quietly and I won't complain, I promise. Just please, please, *please* let me go with them today?"

The doctor hesitated yet again, and put her back to Rosie. "It isn't protocol," she told Grant and Rena, "but let me see what I can do." Starting for the door, she added, "Will you two be all right here?"

Rena put a protective arm around Rosie. "Of course we will." Again, she did her best to ignore the child's rigid response to her touch. Somehow, since learning that her parents weren't dead after all, she must have come up with her own conclusion: Her dad wasn't to blame for her mother's mistake.

"I shouldn't be long," Robson said, leaving them.

"So, Rosie," Grant said, hands on knees, "how 'bout if you show Mom and me what you've been working on over there."

Rosie took his hand, led him to the bright blue rug where she'd constructed her blocks castle. "This," she said, "is where the king lives."

Grant also sat cross-legged on the floor. "Yes, yes I see. That's some castle you've made!"

Rena joined them, put a fingertip on the flat blue blocks that surrounded the building. "Is this the moat?"

"Mm-hmm," the girl muttered.

She'd had no difficulty making eye contact with Grant. *If only she'd look at me,* Rena thought, *she'd see how much I love her!* She set aside her hurt feelings and pressed on. "Which room is the king in?"

Pointing at a chunky, lopsided turret, she said, "He's in there. That's where the queen is, and the princess, too." She met Rena's eyes with a flat, unfeeling stare. "*They* never, *ever* leave their little girl alone because they know there are bad people on the other side of the moat, people who might take her far, far away."

Was it her way of letting them know that life with Barbara hadn't been the pretty picture she'd painted for Robson?

Rena made up her mind to do everything in her power to break through the icy wall between her and Rosie.

Rena sat back on her heels, watching as Grant and Rosie added a wing to the castle. An ugly thought surfaced: what if the only way to ensure Rosie's well-being was to remove herself from the family circle?

CHAPTER SEVEN

"WHY CAN'T I sit up front, Dad?"

"Because it's dangerous. And if a policeman saw you up here, I'd get a ticket. You have to be in your safety seat. It's the law."

"I think that's a stupid law," Rosie said, kicking the back of Rena's seat. "These things are uncomfortable, and besides, kids get hurt all the time, sitting in them."

"Well," Rena said, doing her best to sound calm and in charge, "I'm sure it is uncomfortable, being belted into it, but until you're older and taller, we'll follow the rules. Dad and I want you to be safe because we love you more than life itself."

Under her breath, Rosie said "Well, *Dad* does, anyway." After a moment of silence she added, "I *hate* this seat!"

Rena stared out the passenger window at the blur of cars, pickups and semis that whizzed by on I-90. She couldn't give in. She wouldn't quit, no matter how difficult Rosie tried to make it. *She* was the grown-up, and she had to set aside her hurt feelings.

"Fortunately, you won't be in it much longer. We'll be at the hotel before you know it."

The girl exhaled a loud sigh. "I'm hungry."

"How 'bout pizza?" Grant asked.

"I *love* pizza. Pepperoni and mushroom!"

Rena typed "pizza near Hilton O'Hare" into her phone as Rosie kicked the back of her seat again.

"I'll put in an order," she said. "Remind me which street our hotel is on?" she said to Grant.

"You forget stuff a lot, don't you?" Rosie asked.

Grant chanced a quick glance over his right shoulder. "Rosie, don't talk to your mom that way, okay?"

"It's all right," Rena said. "It's been a couple of long, harrowing days. She's tired and afraid."

"I am *not* afraid, 'cause my *daddy* will

protect me." Pausing, she added, "Won't you, Daddy."

"You know it. And so will your mom."

Rena ignored Rosie's loud sigh and dialed the pizza place. She had to give Grant points for sticking up for her. Since her arrival from Fenwick Island, he'd been accommodating, in an arm's-length kind of way. Even that level of tolerance had to be difficult for the man who still blamed her for Rosie's disappearance. Her mom liked to say "Count your blessings where they grow," and for the first time, Rena understood it in a very personal way.

After placing their order, Rena disconnected. "It'll be half an hour. Just long enough to give us time to settle in."

"Did I used to like pepperoni and mushrooms on my pizza?" Rosie piped up from the back seat.

"You loved it," Rena told her. "So much that if we didn't keep a close eye on you, you'd pick all the toppings off our slices and put them on yours!"

"My other mom made her own pizzas. Sometimes she let me help knead the dough and spread the sauce on top." She didn't speak for a minute or two, and neither did they.

"You know what, Dad?"

"What…"

"I don't remember what pepperoni and mushroom tastes like."

"Then it's a good thing your mom has a good memory, isn't it."

Rena didn't need to turn around to know how Rosie had reacted to that. She pictured the slightly pursed lips and tucked-in corner of her mouth. She'd probably crossed both arms over her chest, too.

The little family remained quiet for the final minutes of the drive. In the hotel parking lot, as Grant hefted the small bag of clothes provided by the foster care system, Rena reached for Rosie's hand and gently tugged her close. "People like that make me so mad," she said, glaring at a speeding SUV. "What's he thinking, driving so fast in a parking lot!"

Rosie's stony expression didn't soften, but at least she hadn't jerked back her hand.

Rena noted the frayed sleeves of her

daughter's sweatshirt jacket. Loose threads caused one pocket to droop. And the cord in the hood was missing.

"First chance we get, we'll go shopping, buy you all new clothes and shoes and—"

"Daddy," Rosie said, letting go to grasp Grant's hand, "can you take me, instead?"

"I don't know the first thing about girls' clothes." While Rosie pushed the elevator's Up button, he met Rena's eyes. "Sorry," he mouthed.

Rena answered with a helpless shrug as Rosie said, "Well, can you come with us?"

"I'd be bored. So bored, I'd fall asleep standing up."

Rosie giggled. "Like a horse?"

Grant whinnied then tousled her hair. "Either that, or I'd end up snoring on the floor, and you and your mom would have to drag me out to the car."

Grinning up at him, she said, "*That* won't happen."

"Why not?"

"Because! You're way too big for us to drag anywhere. But…" She looked at Rena.

"We wouldn't leave him alone, not even for a minute, would we, Mom."

She called me Mom*!* Heart hammering with relief, Rena pushed fearful thoughts and worries from her mind. She wanted nothing more than to wrap her in a fierce hug—and feel Rosie return it—but she resisted. All in good time, she told herself.

The elevator doors hissed open, and the VanMeters stepped inside.

"My other mother didn't like elevators, so we always took the stairs," Rosie announced. "But I remember the time when I broke my arm." She looked up at Grant. "Remember? When the doctor sent us upstairs for X-rays?"

"How could I forget! You scared the life out of me that day. If it hadn't been for Mom's quick thinking, who knows how long it would have taken me to pull myself together and drive us to the ER."

Good one, Rena thought. But not good enough, as evidenced by the doubt on Rosie's face.

They reached their floor, and Rosie followed close on Grant's heels as he led the way down the hall. She stood so near his elbow as he pushed the keycard into its slot that Rena wondered how he'd managed to avoid poking her temple.

He flicked on the lights, and Rosie bounded into the room. "Ooh, a flat-screen TV! Which bed is mine?"

"It's up to you," Rena said. While they ate pizza, she'd think of a reason to sleep on the cot.

Rosie chose the bed nearest the window.

"Let me turn down the covers for you," Rena said. "Even in a nice hotel like this one, you can't be sure how long it's been since they last washed the bedding."

Rosie's shoulders slumped. "Dad, tell me she's not always this picky."

"Mom isn't being picky. She's just looking out for you. Because she loves you."

Rosie met Rena's eyes, her expression saying what words needn't: *Yeah? So where were you when my other mother took me away?*

"How about a quick shower while we're waiting for the pizza?" Rena suggested. "Then you can get into your PJs and slide under the covers and watch some TV while you eat, all warm and snuggly."

"Snuggly? I'm not a baby, you know. And anyways, I took a shower at the Millers' this morning." She pointed at the folded-up cot near the door. "What's that thing for?"

Grant slapped a hand to the back of his neck. It's what he'd always done when frustration got the better of him. Robson had warned them that Rosie's behavior might be less than ideal as she grappled with her new circumstances, yet the two of them had no power to do anything about it. At least, not yet.

"It's one of those just-in-case things," Grant told her. "I'm a restless sleeper. So if I get to tossing and turning, Mom can sleep on the cot."

Rosie looked suspicious.

"I snore, too, so…"

Rena had no memory of him tossing and turning. Or snoring, for that matter. He'd given her the perfect excuse to get out of sharing the bed. Either that, or it was his polite way of saying he wouldn't mind one last night alone.

Rena had slept in the bed nearest the window last night. Once they got back to the house, Rosie would expect them to sleep in the same bed. *Might as well rip off the Band-Aid.*

The image of him in his usual nighttime attire, boxer shorts and a T-shirt, brought back so many happy memories. Rena had often teased him, saying he could wear oil-streaked coveralls and look handsome.

Get hold of yourself, you ninny. What she needed, Rena decided, was a distraction. Reaching into her purse, she withdrew a packet of disinfectant wipes and proceeded to clean the remote control, the doorknobs, the light switches. While in the bathroom wiping the faucet, toilet handle and vanity, she heard Rosie's quiet voice: "Does she do stuff like this all the time?"

Rena tensed.

"Look at it this way, Rosie-girl. If the people who rented the room before us were sick, we could get sick, too. Mom's just looking out for us. It's what she does." He paused, then added, "I think that's pretty nice, don't you?"

Instead of answering his question, Rosie said, "Will you read to me?"

"Sure, but how 'bout you take that shower and get into your PJs first."

Rena exited the bathroom and went directly to Rosie's bag. The hearts-and-flowers pajamas she'd bought looked two sizes too big. The cuffs were frayed, and a button was missing. She held them to her face, relieved that at least they smelled clean.

"Here you go, sweetie," she said, placing them on the bed.

Rosie gathered them to her chest and headed for the bathroom. "And in case you're wondering, I don't need any help, because I'm *not* a baby." With that, she closed and locked the door.

Rena slumped onto the foot of the bed and massaged her temples. "Dr. Robson said this might be difficult, but I had no idea it'd be *this* difficult." She met Grant's eyes. "Rosie hates me."

He sat beside her. "Nah. She's just confused. Barbara's gone, and she's been shuttled from the mall to the police station to the FBI to Robson's office, with a foster home in between. And let's not forget that until a couple days ago, she thought we were dead."

"You're right, of course. *I* can barely make sense of it all, and I'm not nine years old."

There was a knock on the door. Grant rose slowly, saying, "Give her time, Rena. She'll come around."

He placed both pizza boxes on the low-slung bureau beside the TV cabinet then rapped on the bathroom door. "Pizza's here, sweetie. C'mon out before it gets cold."

"Okay, Dad." Rosie emerged a moment later in her oversized PJs. "Did Mrs. Miller pack my toothbrush?"

Rena rummaged through the bag and found it. "Yes, she did, but I don't see toothpaste. It's okay. I brought plenty."

The child took care not to touch Rena when accepting the toothbrush. She looked at Grant. "Do you have some, or do you have to use hers, too?"

He'd packed his own bag. Of course he had toothpaste.

Placing a hand atop her head, he winked. "When we get home, we'll get you your own tube, but for now, it's okay to share. We're a family, kiddo, and families share things."

Rena quickly found her toothpaste.

Rosie rolled her eyes. "All right," she said, hand extended. "But I think it's weird to shower and brush my teeth before we eat. Really weird." One slender shoulder rose. "I guess I'd be looking for things to say if I was you, too." She held out her hand, and waited for Rena to give her the toothpaste.

Instead of giving it to her, Rena put it on the vanity counter. Granted, the child had been through a lot. That didn't make it any easier to pretend the disrespect didn't bother her. Perhaps her behavior would improve once Rosie was home, surrounded by familiar things. *A gal can hope...*

She got busy setting the small round table near the window. There were only two chairs, so Rena placed her own paper plate, napkin and soda on Rosie's nightstand. The distance between the bed and the table couldn't be more than three feet. Enough to satisfy Rosie, who'd been working hard at keeping a careful distance.

She let you hold her hand in the parking

lot. And she called you Mom. That's a good start...right?

Grant found an animated movie on TV and kept Rosie distracted by mimicking the characters' voices. Hearing her sweet, little-girl giggles did Rena's heart good. She enjoyed seeing her husband happy and having fun, too. The poor guy had been sad far too long.

Rosie devoured two big slices of pizza and half an apple tartlet. Then, stretching, she said around a yawn, "Now will you read to me, Daddy?"

"You bet I will, kiddo. Where's your book?"

She slid a tattered copy of *The Velveteen Rabbit* from her satchel, and after handing it to him, climbed under the covers. She patted the space beside her. "Sit right here, so I can see the pictures."

Grant toed off his shoes and obliged her.

Rena turned off the TV and cleaned up the pizza mess as Grant read, content to listen as his melodic baritone filled the room.

"Remind me...what's charming mean?" Rosie asked when the word came up.

Rena thought she detected something sly in Rosie's tone, but Grant handled it well. He rubbed his chin and said "It has a couple of meanings, actually. Sometimes it means delightful and pleasant, sometimes it means a person is likeable, or good-looking. Adorable, even!"

Rosie smiled up at him. "Just as I thought. *You're* charming."

He gave her a sideways hug. "Thanks, kiddo." He chucked her chin. "You're pretty charming, yourself."

Rosie turned the page. "My…my other mother only read to me *if* I did all my chores and got all the right answers on my homework. I hated when she gave math homework. I'm not very good at math."

According to the file, Rosie had been homeschooled. Rena wondered if Barbara had been a good teacher.

"Your mom is a math whiz. It's one of the reasons she's such a great nurse," Grant said. "She's an excellent teacher, too, so I'm sure she'd love to help you with your school work."

As Rena tossed napkins and paper plates

into the trash can, she felt Rosie's eyes on her. Should she chime in and offer to work with Rosie? Or was it smarter to pretend she hadn't overheard the conversation, and avoid another cold-as-ice confrontation?

"Well? Would you do that?" Rosie prompted.

Rena hesitated. *Just dive in, you 'fraidy cat.* From the moment she and had Grant walked into the playroom, the girl had let dozens of zingers fly. Rena had earned them, and then some. *So what's one more?*

"I'd love that." She wanted to hold Rosie close, to prove how much she meant it. *All in good time,* she told herself.

"Are you going to homeschool me, or can I go to a real school, with other kids and stuff?"

Soon, summer vacation would begin. Rena would make appointments with the principal and guidance counselor at Sentinal Lane Elementary, and with one of the therapists Dr. Robson had recommended. In a few weeks, they'd have an answer to that question.

"Your dad and I haven't had a chance to

discuss it yet, but it seems to me that getting you enrolled in—as you put it—a real school, with kids your own age, would be a very good thing."

Using his thumb, Grant marked their page in the book. "I agree, a hundred percent." He gently elbowed Rosie. "How 'bout you, kiddo? What do you think?"

"Oh, I'd *love* that!" She clasped her hands. "Are there other kids in your…I mean, in *our* neighborhood?"

Rena smiled. "As a matter of fact, there are, all walking distance from our house, and I just know they're going to love you!"

"I used to watch kids from my bedroom window. They looked like they were having a lot of fun. My other mother didn't like playdates. She said it messed up the house. But it made me sad."

It made Rena sad, too, but admitting it might make Rosie feel the need to defend the horrid woman. It was bad enough hearing her refer to Barbara as her "other mother."

According to the pediatrician, Rosie showed no signs of having been physically abused or mistreated in any way, and though they still had to wait for the labs to come back, she didn't appear to suffer from any vitamin deficiencies. Barbara hadn't allowed her to socialize with kids her age, but at least she'd provided healthy food and a safe environment. Rosie knew how to read and, as evidenced by the captions on her construction paper drawings, how to write. Whether or not Rosie was on par with other children her age remained to be seen, since Barbara either hadn't kept or had destroyed any records of homeschool lessons and activities.

"Will I be allowed outside to play?"

Rena tensed. Rosie would probably love to visit the O'Brien kids, two doors down, or the Citerony twins, directly across the street. She'd have to bake some cookies, bring a plate to each neighbor. Getting to know them was step one in learning to trust that they'd watch over Rosie. Besides, keeping her in a bubble wouldn't guarantee her safety…

"Sure you can," Rena said, looking to Grant. "They're great kids, around your age, I think. I'm sure you'll all have fun together."

"And they'll be allowed to come into our house, too?"

"That'll be wonderful. I'll even bake cookies for the bunch of you!"

"Oatmeal raisin," Rosie said slowly, her gaze drifting to a spot over Rena's shoulder. "I remember those." She met Rena's eyes. "They were my favorite."

Did she also remember standing on the kitchen step stool, cracking eggs into the mixing bowl? Or Rena, steadying her tiny hands as she added baking powder and vanilla, as she tried to maneuver the big wooden spoon through the thick batter? Rosie had always taken pride in arranging balls of dough in straight rows on the baking sheets, and loved sitting cross-legged on the floor, watching through the oven's window as the cookies turned golden brown.

"I'll tell you what. Once we're all settled in at home, we'll bake a batch, together."

"My other mother didn't let me do things like that. She said the kitchen is a dangerous place for children."

Her expression and posture made it clear that Rosie hadn't approved of the rule. But no matter how she responded, Rena risked destroying the harmony they'd established these past few moments: disagree with Barbara and underscore Rosie's belief that Rena was incapable of keeping her safe; agree and give her daughter the impression that the unreasonable regulations would continue.

"I promise, we'll be very, very careful."

Rosie bobbed her head. "Okay."

How could one upbeat, agreeable word make her so happy she could cry?

Now, yawning and stretching, Rosie leaned into Grant. "Can we finish the story tomorrow, Dad? I'm sleepy."

"Sure thing, kiddo." He placed the book on the nightstand between the beds. "I'm going to have another slice of pizza while your mom tucks you in, all right?"

Rena could have kissed him for that.

"Okay," Rosie repeated, hopping from the bed. "But first, I need to brush my teeth."

She could have kissed him *twice*.

CHAPTER EIGHT

"I DON'T HAVE any floss..."

Rena found hers and handed it to Rosie. "Thanks..."

Rosie's lips had formed the beginning of the word *Mom*. At least, that was the way it looked to Grant. Wishful thinking or not, it gave him hope that the wall between them had begun to crumble.

Sitting on either side of Rosie's bed, he and Rena listened to her prayers and tucked her in. Moments later, when the sounds of her soft, steady breaths told them she was fast asleep, Grant helped himself to one of two leftover slices of pizza.

"Want one?"

Rena shook her head. "No, I'm stuffed. But thanks."

He waved her to their side of the room, and she sat beside him at the foot of the bed.

"Was I imagining things, or did Rosie almost call you mom?" he said quietly.

"I thought I was seeing things! Yes, that's how it looked to me, too."

He bit off the point of the slice. "It's a good sign," he said around it, "especially so early in the...what did Robson call it?" He made air quotes with his free hand. "'The process.'"

"Oh, I hope you're right, Grant. It hurts, knowing she doesn't trust me, but in her shoes, I'd probably feel the same way."

"No you wouldn't."

She shifted to face him, pressing her knee against his thigh. Was that intentional?

"You don't have a mean bone in your body," he continued. "It's what makes you excuse just about every awful thing that's ever happened to you."

"I don't make excuses—"

"Oh, really? What about when the guy at the grocery store put the canned goods on top of the bread, and you said something must have happened to distract him? Or the time the mechanic left loose nuts and bolts, and all the oil drained out of your car? You said maybe he hurt his wrist, and it hurt to tighten them."

"I scolded the girl at the dry cleaners for losing your favorite white shirt…"

"Right. By telling her you realize she doesn't run the operation, single-handedly, *but*…"

Her nose crinkled slightly as she smiled at the memory. He'd always loved it when she did that. If he hadn't been holding the pizza, Grant would have slid an arm around her, pulled her close and kissed her. And knowing Rena, she would have let him, even though he topped the list of people who'd hurt her. She could forgive near-strangers their transgressions, but she had every right to expect better from her husband. He'd promised to love and honor her, to make her feel safe, always.

During those first weeks after Rosie was taken, he'd managed to keep a civil tongue. They were both in shock, after all. But as the months dragged on, and it became clear the cops probably wouldn't find their girl, he'd let some terrible accusations fly. And Rena had taken them all on the chin. When she'd suggested having another baby, he'd called her selfish for using an innocent child to salve her guilty conscience. Didn't she realize, he'd demanded, that even if he agreed—and he did *not*—another child could never replace his sweet girl? His words had cut deep. He knew, because he'd seen the pain in her eyes. And although he'd given her plenty of ammunition to strike back, she hadn't. Following each attack, he'd spent countless hours rationalizing what he'd said, telling himself that Rena never fought back because she agreed with him.

But he knew better. It simply wasn't in her nature to lash out, even in self-defense.

"She'll come around," he said.

"I intend to do everything I can to make that happen, no matter how long it takes or how many bumps there are in the road."

She hadn't said "try." He remembered how frustrating it had been for her to listen to anyone say that word. "Either do a thing, or don't," she'd say.

"I know you will." One more reason to work on loving her again. It shouldn't be all that hard…if he focused on how sweet-tempered and caring she'd always been.

He shook his head. *Get a grip. She's still the person responsible for the five years you lost with your little girl…*

Standing, he dropped the pizza crust into the garbage. "Think I'll get ready for bed. We'll need to get an early start in the morning."

"Right. I hear navigating O'Hare's terminals can be torture."

Not as torturous as wanting her and feeling like he might never truly have her.

He looked over at their sleeping daughter. She seemed so peaceful and happy, so innocent and angelic. Wishful thinking? Or did they have reason to hope that was exactly how Rosie felt, now that she was reunited with them?

He unzipped his bag, removed the deep purple Ravens PJ bottoms, his toothbrush and toothpaste. "I'll only be a minute," he said, stepping into the bathroom. Though he knew it'd be longer than that. Lots longer. He needed time. Time to shelve his resentment and focus, instead, on how hard Rena was trying…

A soft knock at the door ended his reverie.

"I hate to sound cliché, but you didn't fall in, did you?"

Grant opened the door. "Sorry."

"It hasn't been that long, but I didn't hear anything…water running, tooth-brushing… I just wanted to make sure you're all right."

He grasped her wrist and pulled her inside. "Have a seat," he said, gesturing toward the toilet.

She blinked in surprise and then grinned. "Who would have thought you'd put me on the throne!"

"Ha ha. Very funny." He closed the door and leaned against the vanity counter. Arms crossed, Grant said, "I need you to know I'm sorry, Rena."

She swallowed. "Like I said, you haven't been in here all that long."

She knew as well as he did why he'd apologized. It was her sweet way of giving him an out, if he wanted one.

Grant looked at the ceiling, where evidence of a leak had turned the corner tile a sickly shade of yellow. *Good thing Rena hasn't noticed,* he thought, *or she'd figure out a way to get up there and disinfect the thing.* He could almost hear her as she scrubbed away, insisting that they couldn't be too careful.

"What I'm sorry for, Rena, are all the ugly things I've said to you."

Her green eyes widened and sparkled in the fluorescent light. She licked her lips. Took a deep breath. Sat up as tall as her five-foot-two-inch frame would allow. He could hardly blame her for feeling uneasy. The apology had been a long time coming. And she had no reason to believe its sincerity.

"I understand. It's all right," she said slowly, quietly.

"See? There you go again, making excuses for bad behavior."

She stared at her hands, clasped tightly in her lap.

"I just wanted to get that out in the open, so you'll believe me when I say I'm going to work with you on this. We're in it together, for better or worse."

When she met his eyes, Grant held his breath. Oh, to have mind-reading powers. He would give anything to know if she'd zeroed in on his "better or worse" comment. Was she wondering why he hadn't paid more attention to that, years ago?

And did she realize how beautiful she looked, sitting there in her peach-colored dress and matching shoes? If she kept staring at him that way… It made him want to draw her close and kiss away all the sadness and bitterness of the past few years. A lot of water had rushed under the proverbial bridge. Enough water to rock its foundation?

"What did you think about Robson's suggestion, that we tell Rosie the truth?" Grant asked. He'd made his opinion clear, but Rena's lack of response hadn't escaped his notice.

"About our separation? Absolutely not! She isn't ready for another shock, especially not so soon."

"Maybe you're right." He uncapped the toothpaste, squirted a line onto the bristles.

"I'll give you some privacy," she said, opening the bathroom door.

A mere two feet separated them. One sideways step and—

She tiptoed into the hall. "Don't rush on my account. I'm fine."

Grant sped it up anyway. He still had a lot of thinking to do, but he could do it in bed. It wasn't likely he'd sleep at all tonight. A good thing. He needed to figure out how to keep his promise—to cooperate on every level— without taking advantage of her loving, giving character. Or getting hurt himself.

Because much as he'd missed her, much as he loved her, Rena was still the reason he'd lost so many years with his Rosie-girl.

IN THE MOMENTS it took Rena to come fully awake, she didn't know which disturbed her more, Rosie's quiet moans or the distance between her and Grant. She'd grabbed his extra pillow and clutched it to her. A pathetic substitute for his arms?

Rena shook her head and slipped slowly from the bed, wincing when its springs squeaked, and went to her deeply sleeping daughter's side.

A slice of brightness from the parking lot

lights slipped through a gap in the curtains, illuminating one side of Rosie's face. Brow furrowed and lips pursed, she issued another quiet moan.

Rena pulled the covers higher then sat on the edge of the mattress. "What are you dreaming about, sweet girl, to put such a look on your pretty face?" she whispered, finger-combing nearly-blond bangs from the child's forehead.

Rosie's frown deepened as a quiet whimper passed her lips.

"Shh, honey. By this time tomorrow, you'll be home, sleeping in your own bed. No need to worry anymore because your dad and I will take care of you."

Rosie stirred, and Rena froze, concerned that she'd disturbed the girl's much-needed sleep.

Then Rosie extended her arms, as if inviting a hug. And Rena was more than happy to oblige. She lay down beside her and drew her close, pressing tender kisses to her temple, her forehead, her cheek. Snuggling closer, Rosie buried her face in the crook of Rena's neck. The sound of her steady breaths brought thankful tears to her eyes. "Oh, how I love you, Rosie-girl," she said on a sigh.

How ironic, Rena thought, that she and Rosie had both reached out for warmth and comfort during the night. It seemed wrong that Grant had no one to offer the same solace to him.

Then, a startling question surface in her mind: What if Rosie had been reaching out for Barbara? Would it upset her, upon waking, to realize whose arms had cradled her as she slept?

Eyes shut tight, Rena willed the possibility from her mind. Not a difficult feat, if she allowed herself to focus on the treasure wrapped in her arms.

ROSIE MUTTERED QUIETLY in her sleep. If Grant had been sleeping deeply, himself, he probably wouldn't have heard it at all. He looked her way, saw that she lay perfectly still, and decided not to nudge her awake.

Rena rolled close to the edge of the mattress. So close that he caught a whiff of her lavender-scented shampoo. The familiar scent was strangely soothing and took him back to a time when he'd loved the way she smelled, fresh from a shower…and right before they fell asleep in one another's arms. He smiled a bit at another memory… Rena, rolling her eyes at a young couple giving in to a very public display of affection. "They're trying too hard to make others think they're so in love that they can't keep their hands off each other." She'd stood on tiptoe and pressed a light kiss to his cheek. "Aren't we lucky? We show our affection for one another…in private."

She hadn't exaggerated.

Warmth rushed through him. He blamed too much time alone, too many months of missing her for his intense reaction to her nearness. Her fingers, splayed across her pillow, brought back yet another recollection; if things were good between them, that delicate hand would lie on his chest, instead.

She stirred, then stiffened. Probably sensing that she'd inched so close to the edge of her mattress that she risked ending up on his bed. Then, as though his fretfulness had woken her, Rena tossed her covers aside and slid out of bed.

"What are you dreaming about, sweet girl, to put such a look on your pretty face?"

So, he thought, *she'd heard Rosie's whimpers, too...*

Silhouetted as she was by light from the parking lot below, he could see her tuck the covers under their daughter's chin and smooth wayward locks back into place. He couldn't make out what she said next, but there was no mistaking her last words: "...no need to worry anymore, because your dad and I will take care of you."

Then Rosie's arms lifted, and Rena lay down and filled them. He could watch with eyes wide open now because her back was to him. And what a picture! Grant smiled to himself.

Singing softly, Rena stroked their girl's hair. He recognized the tune as one Rosie had asked her mother to sing when she wasn't feeling well.

He'd forgotten what a lovely voice she had, but remembered well that Rena's songs had the power to soothe and calm.

And then all was silent, save the tick of

his wristwatch on the nightstand. *Good,* he thought, *they're both sleeping peacefully.*

It dawned on him that Rena had nothing to keep her warm. He got out of bed and gathered up the blanket from her cot and eased it over her.

She exhaled a soft sigh and snuggled deep into its warmth, momentarily capturing his hand between her chin and the blankets. Oh, how tempting it was to lie down beside her and embrace them both.

Get a grip. What if Rena woke to find him there, and recoiled from his touch? They couldn't risk Rosie seeing something like that.

He needed to get control of his emotions. Otherwise he wasn't sure how he was going to make it through the next days…weeks…

He'd manage. What choice did he have?

"We're not so naïve as to believe this will be easy," she'd told Robson.

Grant scrunched the too-soft pillow and burrowed into it. "When you're right, you're right, Rena," he whispered.

She'd reassured him when upcoming exams left him feeling dumber than a block

of wood, nursed him back to health the year
he came down with pneumonia, tended him
after he'd rolled down a ski slope and broken
his leg. For as long as he'd known her, Rena
had been right there beside him. He'd been
proud to call her his wife, but never more
proud than when she tucked that tiny pink-
blanketed bundle of energy into his arms
that rainy night in May.

Drowsiness settled over him and he closed
his eyes, knowing even before he drifted off
to sleep that she'd be in his dreams.

CHAPTER NINE

FOR DAYS, ROSIE talked about her first-ever plane trip. The minuscule bathroom, the comical guy who taught passengers how to buckle their seat belts, the pretty flight attendant who gave her a faux gold pin. She wore it for more than a week, on T-shirts and sweatshirts, and if Rena hadn't pointed out that the wings could scratch her, Rosie would have worn it to bed, too.

She loved running back and forth between their house and Tina's, usually leaving home with a favorite stuffed animal and returning with cookies, brownies or fudge. During meals, she entertained Grant with knock-knock jokes and silly faces. At bedtime, she amazed them with sweet, childlike prayers, and woke them with an off-key rendition of the "Good Morning" song. And many times a day, she delighted Grant with surprise hugs.

It hurt Rena like crazy, watching Rosie interact with Grant, while sharing none of the sweet gestures with her. Though she pretended not to notice how deliberately Rosie ignored her, Rena was determined to mention her concerns at their first meeting with Dr. Danes.

The psychologist spent forty minutes alone with Rosie, but during the time allotted to her and Grant, Rena grew impatient. Why was he so determined to learn about their childhoods when the only childhood that mattered was Rosie's!

"I can see you have something on your mind, Mrs. VanMeter. Care to talk about it?"

"I just think we should be talking more about Rosie and less about us."

"Good point," Grant said.

Danes nodded. "I see. Anything specific that concerns you?"

"For one thing, Rosie only mentions Barbara to let us know what she cooked, or which books she read to her, that she believed student-teacher ratios in public schools are horrible, that TV is the ruination of today's youth."

Grant said, "Rena is right. Good or bad, Barbara was pretty much the only person Rosie interacted with. Shouldn't she be… shouldn't she be mourning her death?"

Danes nodded thoughtfully. "I'll be honest. That day is coming. No doubt about it. But for now, I see no reason to kick up dust."

Rena couldn't believe her ears. "Kick up dust! What does that mean?"

Grant sent her a look that said, *"easy, now."* Their relationship had improved considerably in the past couple weeks, due in large part to Rosie's antics and mostly happy mood. Too often, though, when he thought she wouldn't notice, he watched her through narrowed, suspicious eyes, as if waiting for her to say or do something that might put Rosie in harm's way.

Now he leaned forward. "Sorry if we seem thickheaded, Dr. Danes, but how are we supposed to prevent problems if we don't know what to look for?"

"You can't. Eventually, Rosie will come

to terms with what happened to Barbara.
Children don't cope with grief in the same
way adults do. Add to that the fact that she's
been through a lot of changes in a short period of time. In a word, she's overwhelmed.
She's still processing, learning what does
and doesn't please you, teaching herself
ways to fit in her new environment. Sooner
or later, she'll feel comfortable enough—
and she'll trust you enough—to deal with
her past."

He walked around to the front of his desk
and leaned against it. Rena frowned. What
was it with psychiatrists and their penchant
for *perching*?

Danes removed his glasses. "At that point,
you may see changes in her behavior." He
counted on his fingers. "Spending more time
alone in her room, bursting into tears for no
apparent reason. She might sulk, or lash out
at you. Those will be signs that she has questions, but doesn't know how to ask them."
Using the glasses as a pointer, Danes added,
"That's when you'll need to coax information from her. Not by mentioning Barbara's

death, mind you, because that may not be the cause of the new behavior."

Grant blew a stream of air through his teeth. "Let me get this straight. You're saying we play the waiting game, keep a close eye on her, and if she starts acting out—or even *looks* like that's what she's doing, we get her to talk." He slapped a hand to the back of his neck. "I don't mind telling you, doc, that sounds counterproductive. Why not just sit her down and ask her how she's doing with the whole losing Barbara thing, and deal with it in an honest, straightforward way?"

"My house is for sale," Danes said.

Rena and Grant exchanged a curious glance.

"My Realtor loves to say 'location is everything.' Well, in cases like this, *timing* is everything."

Grant shook his head. "I thought that's what actors said about comedy."

Arms crossed, Danes said, "Mr. Van-Meter, I realize that you and your wife are under a lot of stress, too, but I'm sure you'll agree that our main goal is helping Rosie deal with her past and adjust to her present."

Rena knew that look. Grant's frustration had just about reached its height. Any minute now, he'd jump up and leave the office. If that happened, he'd stubbornly refuse to return, which meant finding another therapist. And yet another change that wouldn't be good for Rosie.

"We're just confused," she interjected. "Say too little, Rosie pays the price. Say too much—or at the wrong time…" She extended her hands, palms up. "What we need from you, Dr. Danes, is applicable *advice*. Without that, we might as well flounder around on our own."

The doctor pressed his palms together. "Do you realize what's just happened?"

Again, Rena and Grant exchanged a puzzled look.

"You got back together to present a united front to Rosie, and from what she has told me, it's working." He smiled. "This exchange makes that even more clear. Your reactions show me that you're true partners in this."

Partners. Would she and Grant find their way back to the beginning, when they'd been that for each other? Or had too many hurts and disappointments, too many harsh words and resentments ruined what they'd had? They'd shared a few lighthearted family moments since Rosie's return, and yet, crossing that bridge seemed an unlikely dream…until the memory of Grant, tenderly covering her with the comforter, surfaced.

Danes returned to his chair, rousing her from the daydream.

"She's going to be fine," he said, "with you two looking out for her." He tapped his watch. "On that note…"

This was Rena's chance. "I have another question, Doctor. It's about the way Rosie has been treating me. She isn't rude, exactly, but for the most part, she pretty much ignores me. Do you feel, as I do, that it's because she blames me for the kidnapping?"

Danes frowned. "It's definitely possible. Although, it might give you some relief to know she didn't say anything of that sort when I spoke with her."

Rena didn't understand, and said so.

"When I asked how you two are getting along, she told me you're a hard-working mother, preparing meals, keeping the house and yard tidy, making sure she wears clothing that's appropriate for the weather." He paused, his frown deepening. "I suppose that could mean that Rosie realizes it isn't in her best interest to point out any negatives about you."

"That's what it *could* mean?" Grant scowled.

"You've noticed this behavior, too?"

"I'd have to be deaf and blind *not* to have noticed, Doc."

"And what are you doing to make your wife a part of things that you and Rosie do?"

Now, he looked annoyed. Because he didn't believe he should be responsible for Rosie's behavior? Or because he felt bad that he hadn't done enough to include Rena?

In place of an answer, Grant stood and made his way to the door.

"Will we find Rosie in the playroom?" he asked.

"Yes. She's with Meredith, who's conducting a few tests. Soon as I've had a chance to study the results, she and I will devise an action plan. I'll call you so we can discuss how I believe we should proceed."

Muttering something about plans and proceedings, Grant walked into the playroom. The doctor stared after him in bewilderment. *Why should we be the only ones who are confused?* Rena thought. It seemed a shame Grant hadn't been there to enjoy the moment.

"Same time next week?" she asked.

"I'll have Meredith call you with some days and times." He patted her shoulder. "Don't worry, Mrs. VanMeter. Rosie is going to be fine. Barbara did a terrible thing, taking her from you—there's no getting around that. But it appears she did a fair-to-middlin' job of caring for her. Resent her if you must—that's a normal reaction—but at the same time, acknowledge that things could have been a whole lot worse."

A myriad of dark possibilities flitted through Rena's brain. Danes was right. Rosie had come home to them without any obvious physical or mental scars. Rena's loathing for Barbara lessened slightly.

Danes nodded toward Grant and Rosie. "Your family is waiting for you…"

Her family. Oh, how she loved the sound of that! Rena looked over her shoulder and saw them, standing hand in hand, Grant grinning and Rosie doing her best to fake a smile.

DANES MUST HAVE mentioned something about school during his meeting with Rosie, because the whole way home, she asked about Sentinal Lane Elementary.

"Do they have sports, like soccer and softball?"

"I don't know, but we'll ask when we're getting you signed up." Rena had done some online research and learned there would likely be tests to determine whether Rosie belonged in fourth or fifth grade. Athletics hadn't even crossed her mind.

"What about music? My other mother said music is important for developing minds."

"Yes, I'm sure the music department is very active. When I've passed Sentinal on my way to the grocery store, I've seen announcements on the marquee for choral recitals and stage plays. We'll get more details when we meet with your principal and guidance counselor."

"What are their names?"

"Mrs. Kingston and Ms. Gilmore."

Rosie nodded. "Mrs. Kingston is the principal?"

Rena smiled. "Yes, honey."

"I want to make a good first impression."

She wondered what had inspired Rosie's *other mother* to teach her that.

"Isn't this Friday?" Rosie asked, seemingly changing the subject.

"Right up until midnight," Grant said.

"Can we have movie night, like I had with my other mother?"

This was the third Friday she'd been back with them. Rena was torn between relief that Rosie felt comfortable enough to bring up the topic, and rancor toward Barbara for depriving them of dozens of Friday nights together.

"Tell you what," she said, facing the back seat. "We'll all get into our pajamas, and while you choose the movie, I'll make popcorn and hot chocolate."

"What will Dad do?"

"I'll turn out the lights, so the family room will feel like a movie theater."

Rosie clapped her hands. "Oh, goodie! I can hardly wait for it to get dark!"

Her behavior and word choices made it hard to believe Rosie had just turned nine. It did Rena's heart good to witness this moment of little-girl glee.

"What is it, sweetie?"

"Does it hurt your feelings when I call Barbara my other mother?"

It hurt like crazy, but Rena couldn't risk damaging the moment of rapport by admitting it.

"You spent a long time with Barbara," she said carefully. "It's going to take a long time to adjust to life without her."

From the corner of her eye, Rena could see her nodding thoughtfully. Would it have been smarter to simply say yes? Maybe Rosie was testing her.

"What if I don't want to get over losing her? What if I'm glad she's gone?"

The question took Rena by surprise.

Grant, too, judging by the bulging muscles in his jaw.

"She liked to say 'I'm strict but fair,'" Rosie said.

"Discipline is a good thing," Grant mused. "When it's rooted in love."

Was it a good thing that Rosie had been referring to Barbara in the past tense? Did it mean she'd soon open up about the day her "other mother" had died? She'd been right beside the woman, after all, saw and heard everything. And her young life had been a dizzying whirlwind ever since.

Thoughts of Barbara and Rosie's talk of school made Rena wonder if the woman had kept up with Rosie's inoculations. The authorities hadn't found any paperwork to indicate that she had. First thing Monday morning, Rena would call their pediatrician to make an appointment. Next, she'd call the school, too, and make arrangements for her and Rosie to meet the principal and guidance counselor.

Grant planned to go back to work on Monday. To this point, he'd been front and center with Rosie while Rena did laundry, ran the vacuum, prepared meals. Rena had come to rely on him—for time spent with their daughter and the countless other things he'd done to smooth Rosie's transition—and was surprised to realize that she'd miss having him around.

It seemed Grant appreciated the way she'd shouldered the chores, giving him more time to spend with Rosie. What would he think if he knew that house and yardwork had provided convenient reasons to avoid watching their warm interactions?

Rena had one weekend to figure out another strategy. If not, come Monday, she'd be spending all day alone with a daughter who couldn't even offer her a genuine smile.

CHAPTER TEN

"THAT MOVIE WAS so silly. Better than anything I watched with my other mother."

Rena fluffed Rosie's pillow and tried not
to let her disappointment show. It made
sense that Rosie would have the woman on
her mind. Life with Barbara was the only
reality Rosie had known for five years. But
that didn't stop the references from hurt-
ing Rena. "I'm glad you had fun," she said,
pressing a kiss to her forehead.

She tried to ignore the way Rosie turned
her head and winced at the affectionate gesture.

Grant leaned in to kiss Rosie's cheek.
"Ready to say your bedtime prayers?"

She sat up and, eyes closed tight, folded
her hands.

"Five little angels around my bed, one at

the foot and one at the head, one to sing and one to pray, and one to take my fears away."

She'd been two when Rena helped her memorize this one. It hadn't been difficult, because Rosie liked the image of five pretty angels fluttering around her room. Before tonight, she'd recited the "Now I lay me down" prayer that Barbara had preferred. Reason to hope the wall between them was weakening?

"God bless Dad," Rosie continued, "and Grandma. And if you see my other mother, tell her if she's still afraid of the dark, she should talk to the angels. Amen." She lay back on her pillow.

Grant's sympathetic expression didn't do a thing to ease the sting.

"And…" he coaxed.

"Oh. Right. I forgot." She sat up again to add, "Bless Mom, too."

Rena hoped Rosie really had forgotten. Yes, that would hurt, but not nearly as much as knowing she'd intentionally left her off the list.

Isn't going to be easy, convincing her she can rely on me…

Did lack of trust explain the girl's arm's-length attitude, or was something more sinister at work? What exactly had Barbara told her?

Rena put aside her concerns and sat beside Rosie. Sliding an arm across her shoulders, she fought tears and said, "Your dad and I are so lucky to have such a sweet and thoughtful daughter."

"Mmm-hmm," she responded and plopped onto the pillow again before reaching for Grant's hand. "'Night, Daddy."

He kissed her forehead. "'Night, sweet girl."

After turning out the light, Rena lingered in the doorway while Grant headed downstairs. "Would you like your door open or closed, sweetie?"

Rosie rolled over and said, "Whatever you want."

Rena pulled the door shut and, sitting on the top step, held her head in her hands. She needed to get control of herself. Find some way to—how did her dad put it?—take it on the chin. *Time to grow a spine, Ree...* Besides, she couldn't just fall apart and put

Grant in the untenable position of comforting her. Things would get better in time, with patience. They had to.

She puttered in the kitchen for a few minutes before joining Grant in the family room. He'd stretched out on the couch, one long leg slung over the seatback, one arm crooked under his neck.

"We can watch something else," he said without looking away from the screen.

She held up a book. "No, I like watching the O's."

"You okay?"

"Yes, of course."

"She was pretty rough on you up there."

"Not really. She's going through a lot. I just need to be patient. Prove to her that I'll never—"

He sat up, raised his right hand. "You're right. Time and patience is what the doctor ordered."

Please, she thought, *don't start quoting Dr. Danes* already.

"You were right, you know," he said, muting the TV, "that what we need from that

Danes is solid, workable advice, not a bunch of psychological double-speak."

Closing the book, she met his gaze. She hadn't done anything *right* in his eyes since before the kidnapping. Rena waited for an explanation.

"It felt kinda good when you put him on the spot." He shook a fist in the air. "Couple of times, I wanted to slug him."

She could relate. The doctor's methods hadn't provided much help or hope. Time and patience, Rena reminded herself.

"I'm glad you didn't."

He raised an eyebrow, and before he had a chance to claim he was kidding, she said, "I forgot to a tuck a packet of tissues into my purse. How would we explain it if he bled all over Rosie's file?"

The eyebrow lowered.

Long before she'd left him for Fenwick Island, Rena had suggested marriage counseling. Grant refused, saying he didn't believe in throwing good money away on some high-priced speculator. It was reason enough not to tell him about her sessions with Martha. She hadn't told Tina, either; why put her in the position of keeping secrets from her son?

"Admittedly," she said carefully, "my experience with therapists is limited, but something tells me his methods are a tad unorthodox."

"I'd hardly call doing nothing unorthodox. Drives me nuts the way these guys string things out just to get that whopping hourly fee."

She couldn't argue with that. Danes wasn't exactly cheap.

"So what were you two talking about right before we left?"

Rena shook her head. "Oh, he was reassuring me that Rosie is going to be fine, thanks in large part to our united front. And that it's okay for me to resent Barbara...provided I keep in mind that she could have done far worse."

Grant leaned forward. "You've gotta be joking."

"That's the gist of it."

"He really expects us to feel *gratitude* toward that witch because, after she kidnapped our kid, she didn't beat or torture her?" He drove his fingers through his hair. "I think *he* needs a shrink."

A small voice filtered down the stairs, putting a halt to their conversation.

"Daddy? I'm thirsty."

Grant looked at Rena.

She answered in his stead. "Be right up, sweetie."

"No, I'll go," Grant told her.

By the time she got to her feet to challenge him on it, he'd disappeared around the corner. Things would never improve if he kept doing things like this. True, Rosie had asked for him, but…maybe if he'd give her the chance to answer their daughter's calls, Rena could make some headway. But how to tell him without widening the gap that separated them?

"A bit of a schemer, that kid of ours." Grant said when he returned. He flopped back down on the couch, crossed one dark-socked ankle over the other and went back to channel surfing. "Would you believe she almost talked me into another story *and* a song?"

He'd always had trouble saying no to her.

But he hadn't been gone long enough to do both. "Which did she get?"

"I sang the first verse of 'You Are My Sunshine.' Figured it was quicker." He buffed his fingernails on his shirt. "I was right, too. She was droopy-eyed before I finished."

"Self-preservation?"

He lifted a shoulder in response, but he gave no indication that he remembered the good-natured debates they used to have about which of them had the most trouble staying in-tune.

"You know I'm teasing, right?" Rena probed.

"Yeah, I guess."

An hour later, after he turned off the TV, Rena got to her feet. Standing beside the couch, she said, "G'night, Grant."

They'd shared some warm and wonderful moments tonight, so warm and wonderful that, without even thinking about it, Rena bent at the waist and kissed him. Just a light brush of her lips against his.

His stiff, wide-eyed reaction told her the kiss had surprised him. She braced herself for what might come next: a small step forward in their relationship...or a big step back.

"Rena... I, ah..."

What made her reach out and lay a hand against his cheek? Fear? Or hope?

Eyes closed, he leaned into her palm, the bristle of his five o'clock shadow warming her palm.

"It's been a long, weird day," he whispered. And as she stepped back, he got to his feet. "I'm beat."

"Yeah, me, too." Her voice was shaking and she hoped he hadn't noticed.

"Need anything before we turn in?"

Want was the better word choice. She wanted him to treat her the way he once had. To take her in his arms and hold her close, and tell her things would get back to normal soon. More than anything, she wanted him to forgive her.

"No, I'm good."

Rena held her breath, waiting for the words she so longed to hear. Instead, she heard the quiet hum of the ceiling fan.

"Well, g'night then," Grant said finally.

She stood, arms limp at her sides, and watched him walk toward the stairs. Cupping her elbows, Rena fought tears, remembering one of her dad's favorite bits of advice: *Only a fool takes unnecessary chances.* She'd taken a big one, reaching out that way.

"Grant?"

He paused on the landing.

"Are you ever sorry that we… Do you wish we hadn't split—"

"I know we need to talk about that, eventually, but not tonight, okay?"

"Sure," she said tentatively.

"Can I ask you a question?"

"Of course. Anything."

"While you were gone, did you…did you see other men?"

"No."

"Never?"

"Never."

"Why not?"

Because I never stopped loving you, that's why!

The silent answer raised a question of her own: Had Grant seen other women? Her dad's advice reverberated in her head, and she kept her mouth shut.

"Good," he said, and climbed the rest of the stairs.

What had he read into her silence? And was there a chance he felt the same way?

Yet another of her dad's sayings popped into her head: *When things seem too good to be true, they usually are.*

"WHAT'S THIS?" ROSIE ASKED, peering into the package.

"The Fenwick Island lighthouse. Your Grandma Cleary sent it to me."

"Is it your birthday?"

Rena laughed. "Not for a few months."

"Then what's it for?"

"She's my mom, and she misses me." Rena placed the lighthouse on the mantel. "I guess she hopes that seeing it will remind me to call her."

"Why not now?"

"Good question." She grabbed the portable phone and started to dial her parents' number. It had been a week since she'd last spoken to them; her mom was dying to see

Rosie. "On second thought," she said, returning the handset to its charger, "I'll call later, maybe invite them for the weekend. But I want to talk to your dad first to see if he's okay with it."

"Why? Doesn't he like them anymore?"

Anymore…meaning since the kidnapping? "Of course he likes them, and they like him, too." Not the whole truth; her parents had called Grant everything *but* her husband for the way he'd treated her. But Rosie didn't need to know that. And neither did he.

"This is our house—Dad's and yours and mine—and we need to be in agreement about things like that because…"

"I know, I know. It's what *families* do," Rosie said with a hint of impatience. "I remember Grandma Cleary. She always made the best chocolate cake. Didn't she used to get on the floor to help me put my puzzles together?"

Why the emphasis on family? Rena wondered, even as it lifted her spirits to learn that Rosie's memories of her parents were good ones. "Yes, I do. She's more limber than me!"

"Well, I want to see them, so two against one."

Rena tried not to make too much of the thrill she felt, hearing Rosie side with her for once. It didn't mean Rosie saw the two of them as a team, or that she'd stopped blaming Rena for the kidnapping. For all Rena knew, it was a test to see if she'd go against Grant. The psychologist had alerted them to the possibility that Rosie might attempt to pit her parents against one another to get her own way.

"Things don't work that way in a family."

A tiny smile lifted the corners of Rosie's mouth. Rena didn't know how to read that, either.

"Are you going to call Dad or not?"

While living on Fenwick Island, she'd seen her folks several times a week; since moving home three weeks ago she hadn't seen them at all. And she missed them.

Grabbing the phone again, Rena said, "Why don't you call your dad then, and after you've brightened his day, you can pass him to me."

Rosie dialed, her smile brightening when he picked up. She told Grant about the package from Grandma Cleary, and mentioned the possibility of a weekend visit, then handed the phone to Rena.

"So a lighthouse, huh? How big is it?"

"Oh, just fourteen, fifteen inches tall. It's pretty. I think I might start a collection. Lighthouses are legendary, after all. Beacons of hope to the lost and weary."

Just like you.

What would she have done without him to help run interference between her and Rosie?

"Sounds good."

"You don't mind if they spend the weekend, then?"

"Not at all. I've always liked your folks. It'll be good seeing them again. Hey, here's an idea…maybe on Sunday we'll have a good old-fashioned family barbecue. See if your brothers can come, and I'll call my sisters. I'll throw some burgers and dogs on the grill, and maybe our moms will whip up some of their best side dishes and desserts."

"Like Tina's apple pie…"

"And your mom's potato salad." He paused. "And maybe you can make your famous baked beans."

If she remembered the recipe after all this time. "Sounds really nice," she told him. "I'll start making calls." The invitation would be the perfect excuse to explain to everyone that she and Grant had decided to reconcile. But could she count on them to help keep up the pretense…for Rosie's sake?

"I'd better go. Have a client meeting in ten minutes and need to review the file." Another pause, and then, "What's for supper?"

"Oven fried chicken, baked potatoes and salad."

"Mmm…"

"See you tonight, then." She'd just given him the perfect opening to say it. But would he? She heard the rustle of paper—he'd opened the file.

"Right. See you tonight, babe," he said before hanging up.

Rena stared at the handset for a second.

How long had it been since he'd called her that? *Years, that's how long!* Heart fluttering, she returned the handset to its charger, telling herself that Grant hadn't meant it. He'd only said it because he'd been distracted, fallen back into their old routine.

As she'd warned herself the other night, when things seemed too good to be true, they usually were.

CHAPTER ELEVEN

GRANT CARRIED HIS in-laws' suitcases to the guest room. After opening the blinds and adjusting the air conditioner vents, he checked to see if Rena had put fresh towels in the adjoining bathroom. He wasn't surprised to see that she had, but wished she hadn't. Doing the job himself would have killed a few more minutes before he had to join them downstairs.

Since the separation, he'd had no contact with the Reynolds. Grant had no idea how much Rena had told her folks about her reasons for moving to move to Fenwick Island, but if their standoffish attitudes were any indicator, the couple that had been like second parents to him had crossed him off their favorite son-in-law list.

No surprise there. Didn't all parents take their kid's side? He got that. But it wouldn't make it any easier to deal with the couple who probably saw him as the unreasonable bully who had driven their daughter from her own home. If that was how they felt, Grant could hardly blame them; from time to time, he felt the same way.

Kent, Linda, Rosie and Rena were sipping iced tea at the kitchen table when he joined them.

"Everything all right?" Kent asked.

"Sure. Fine. Why?"

"Took you a while to stand a couple of suitcases into the room. I thought maybe one of them had fallen open. Linda has a tendency to overpack."

He ignored the man's suspicious tone and sat between Rosie and Rena. "Nothing like that. Just thought I'd check to see if you had clean towels, an extra blanket, stuff like that. But Rena had already taken care of everything."

"That's our girl," Linda said.

Rena went to the fridge for the pitcher of iced tea and filled a glass for him. "Help yourself to one of your mom's brownies," she said, sitting beside him again. "She brought them over this morning."

"She's coming tonight, though, right?"

"Grandma made brownies for her meeting, and saved a few for us. She's bringing pie tonight," Rosie explained.

Grant breathed a silent sigh of relief. At least he'd have one guest in his corner.

"So, Grant," Kent said. "How are things down at the office?"

He might as well have been talking to someone he'd just met at a cocktail party, instead of the guy who'd married his daughter.

"Great. Fine. Added a new associate to handle the growing client load. Hired a full-time receptionist, too."

"I hope the other partners aren't working you too hard." Linda looked at Rosie. "You're needed at home more than ever, you know."

"No place I'd rather be," he admitted. "But we still need to pay the bills. And we have Rosie's college tuition to think of, of course. Rena and I decided it's best if she stays home, for a while anyway. And I agree."

"Oh, so do I," Linda said. She blanketed Rosie's hand with her own. "This little angel deserves all the one-on-one she can get."

"What's one-on-one?" Rosie wanted to know.

"Time and attention," Grant explained.

"Why do I deserve that?"

Because she'd been stolen from them, kept from them for years. And now that she was home, they'd deliver love, time and attention in spades for the rest of her life. No matter how uncomfortable it was for them.

He draped an arm across the back of her chair. "You deserve it, Rosie-girl, because from the moment you were born, Mom and I have seen you as a gift from heaven, and we love you more than life itself."

During those first harrowing days after her return, she'd looked at Rena with cold indifference. She flashed that same vacant stare in her grandmother's direction now, and peripheral vision told him that Rena had seen it, too. Was she placing some of the blame for what happened at the zoo on Rena's mother...wondering if the woman had done a better job, Rena would have, too?

Had Dr. Robson been right, that clearing the air about the kidnapping, about her years with Barbara, would be good for Rosie? Grant didn't think so. But even if the psychiatrist's assessment had been accurate, this was neither the time nor the place to do it.

Rosie leaned her head on his shoulder, and he moved his arm from the chair back to her shoulders.

"I never forgot you, you know." She flicked a quick look in Rena's direction. "Either of you."

Rena, eyes closed, exhaled a brief sigh. "That's good to hear, sweetie."

Her wavering voice told Grant that Rena was trying to stifle tears.

Linda got up, added ice to her glass. "Can I get anything for anyone else?"

"I'm good," Kent said. "Don't want to spoil my appetite. My taste buds are achin' for a hot dog. Haven't had one since last summer."

"You asked for beanies and weenies just last week," Linda corrected. Her nervous smile did little to mask her discomfort.

"Few things beat a hot-off-the-grill dog."

He winked at his granddaughter. "Isn't that right, Rosie!"

She sent him a shy smile and said, "Right."

"I hope you chopped plenty of onions," he told Rena.

"Don't worry, Dad. I remember what you like."

"You have sweet pickle relish?"

"Yup. And spicy brown mustard, too."

"Good girl!" Eyes on Rosie again, he added, "What say you 'n me go out back and put that ol' swing set to the test."

Rosie turned to Rena. "Can we?"

"Sure."

He knew this woman almost as well as he knew himself. She wanted to draw Rosie close and dot that sweet face with kisses. He would have bet his next paycheck on it.

"Just don't swing too high, okay?" Rena said instead.

"Party pooper," Kent said, taking Rosie's hand.

"It's hot out there," Linda called after them. "Don't let her get overheated, Kent."

When the door closed behind them, Rena's mother finished her iced tea. "Well," she said, standing, "I think I'll go upstairs and hang up a few things."

Yet again, relief rushed through Grant. "Make yourself at home. If you need anything, just whistle."

And now it was just the two of them in the quiet kitchen.

Rena dumped ice cubes into the sink, then stood the glasses on the dishwasher's top rack. "That was a little too close for comfort."

"Yeah. I was thinking the same thing."

"I've tried to keep them up on things without going into too much detail." She slid the pitcher back into the fridge. "No sense giving them more to worry about than necessary."

"Think they caught that look Rosie gave you?"

She hung her head. "If they did, you can bet Mom will ask me about it, first chance she gets."

"You're probably right." He joined her at the sink and rested his hand on hers. "Then I promise not to leave you two alone." He gave her hand a little squeeze. "Not even for a minute."

Grant tamped the urge to kiss her lips. These past few days, she'd seemed a little distant. Near as he could figure, the change—from cheerful to quiet—began that night when she'd kissed him. He hadn't been expecting it, and blamed that for his less than enthusiastic reaction. Still…too much, too soon? Or had the moment of closeness—and his lack of response—made her realize it was too little, too late?

"WHEN DO YOU want me to start the grill?"

She glanced at the clock above the sink. "I need to put a tablecloth on the deck table and make some lemonade. I forget, how long does it take to warm up the grill?"

Rena knew the answer to that as well as he did. Until the separation, she'd been the grill master of the house.

"Ten, maybe fifteen minutes. I haven't had the cover off the thing in years. Guess I should make sure we have enough propane."

"And that nothing has decided to call it

home," Rena added. "Remember the year wasps built a huge nest on the grates?"

"How could I forget? I felt like a pincushion for a week afterward."

She remembered well how long it took to dot anti-sting medication on each welt. "You were covered with red welts. Good thing you're not allergic."

He opened the pantry door and scanned the shelves for his barbecue tools, then around the doorframe. "Where's the burger flipper? And dog tongs?"

She placed buns on a tray, added napkins, ceramic plates and silverware. "Hanging on the wall beside the light switch, I imagine."

Right where they'd been the entire time she was gone, no doubt.

Placing the tools onto the table, he peered into the fridge. "Wow. Potato salad, coleslaw, baked beans..." Straightening, he grinned. "What's this, practice for when we have the whole family over on Sunday?"

"You know me too well."

"I doubt anyone's going to want pizza later. Not after chowing down on all this."

"Popcorn and hot chocolate, then. And if

someone gets a hankering, I have a couple of pizzas in the freezer."

"The little ones that Rosie loved when she was…little?"

It surprised her that he'd remembered. Rena had always reserved those for when he worked late or went out of town on business. "Yes."

He parted the white cotton back door curtains. "She's having a ball out there. Your dad will have sore muscles in the morning, though, after pushing her on that swing all this time." Grant looked toward the stairs. "Guess your mom decided to take a nap."

"A nap?" She clucked her tongue. "Have you *met* my mom? The only time I ever saw her nap, she had a temperature of 102."

One hand on the doorknob, he faced her. "Forgot to tell you. I moved all those bags of stuff you gathered up for the charity truck. Put them in my trunk. Out of sight, out of mind. You know, for your mom's own good."

Last time her parents spent a weekend—years earlier—her mother had given in to her usual urge to snoop. She'd peeked into the upstairs hall closet, where Grant had stacked storage bins and boxes of Christmas decorations. A loud clatter brought them running from opposite sides of the house. No one, not Kent or Grant, not even two-and-a-half-year-old Rosie had believed her when she said, "I thought I saw a mouse..."

"Good. Thanks." Rena had spent every evening collecting items for donation. She'd thought clearing old stuff out of the house would help give them all a fresh start—and the task was proving to be a good excuse to keep a safe distance between her and Grant after Rosie had gone to bed.

He opened the door, and she stopped him with "Grant?"

"Yeah?"

"Is it just me, or does Rosie seem a little... quieter than usual?"

"Ah. Because of that look earlier?"

She shivered at the memory of it. "Yes, that. But for the past couple of days, I've noticed her just sitting, staring into space, no emotion on her face at all. Once, I walked past her bedroom and she was lying on the floor, hugging Mr. Fuzzbottom and gaping at the ceiling."

"Now that you mention it," he said, "I caught her stomping around the pool, fist-punching the air, looking like she was mad at the world. When I asked her why, she got this guilty look on her face and said, 'I hate mosquitos.'"

It might mean nothing. Rena *hoped* it meant nothing. But something told her that was too much to expect. "Maybe the other shoe is about to drop."

"Rena." He dropped his big, gentle hand onto her shoulder. "Quit worrying. She's made it this far. She'll make it the rest of the way, too. Besides, if she needs to vent, well, that's what we're here for, right?"

True enough, but… "I've kept her pretty busy. What if she feels there's no good time to get things off her chest? Or she's too distracted to process?"

He gave her a quick, sideways hug. "Nah. It's good that you've been taking her places, doing things with her. She's settled in here, so well that sometimes, I almost forget…"

Grant's expression changed from warm and understanding to cool and emotionless. He made his way back to the door.

She handed him the iced tea pitcher. "Can you carry that out for me? I'll bring some plastic cups out in a minute, in case they're thirsty."

"Sure," he said dully. Then he gathered the grilling tools in his free hand and went outside.

Rena cupped her elbows and hung her head. Since reuniting with Grant and Rosie, she'd rarely entertained the guilty thoughts that had shadowed her all these years. On the occasions when self-blame reared its ugly head, she'd tried to tell herself all that mattered was that Rosie was back. Rena wanted Grant to forgive her, but would she ever forgive herself?

"Not if I live to be a hundred," she muttered.

"What's that, honey?"

"Oh, hi, Mom. Didn't hear you come in." Rena didn't want to talk about the kidnapping, or the years Rosie had been away from them. Or Grant. She hoped a quick hug would distract her mother. "I'm so glad you and Dad are here!"

"We're glad, too."

She had that maternal I've-got-your-number look on her face, so Rena quickly added, "Did you find everything you needed up there?"

"Yes. And the room is just as lovely as I remembered it. Nothing like big windows and a southern view, you know?"

Rena smiled and opened a kitchen drawer, pulled out a red-and-white checkered tablecloth. "Soon as I plate up the hot dogs and hamburgers for Grant, we'll set the table."

"All right." Her mother lifted her chin. "But I have to say, you're not fooling me, young lady."

"Fooling you? What do you mean?"

"We'll talk about it later. We wouldn't want to start anything we can't finish, now would we?"

Unless she was mistaken, the two of them would be up late tonight. Rena needed to come up with something to tell her that would allay her suspicions about the reconciliation.

Hiding her face in the fridge, Rena took her time gathering the hot dogs and the burgers she'd pattied earlier. Placing both on the counter, she said, "There's a serving tray on the bottom shelf of the pantry. Would you mind getting it for me?"

Linda sighed. "All right," she said again.

And thankfully, that was all she said.

Balancing the tray on one hip, Rena opened the door and was met by her teary-eyed daughter. Kent and Grant hovered nearby as Rena slid the tray onto the counter and got onto her knees.

"Rosie, sweetie, what's wrong?"

"I-I-I got a-a sliver!" she cried, holding up one thumb.

Rena cradled Rosie's small hand in hers and inspected the injury. With a little luck, the child wouldn't notice Rena's own hand trembling. It worried her that Rosie seemed near-hysterical over a little splinter. She'd always been a calm kid. Tears, yes. But sobbing? *"The kid is tough as nails,"* Grant used to say when she skinned a knee or stubbed a toe.

"It's okay, sweetie. Just a tiny wood chip, and it's easy to see. Getting it out will be easy as pie." She got to her feet. "C'mon," she said, taking Rosie's other hand, "let's get you all fixed up."

She led Rosie into the powder room and sat her down on the toilet seat as Grant and her parents gathered in the hall. After placing a towel on the girl's lap, Rena dampened a washcloth and gently blotted her daughter's tears. Then, unscrewing the cap on the peroxide bottle, she said, "This might sting a little. Close your eyes tight and hold your breath…"

Rosie's nose wrinkled and her brow furrowed as Rena dribbled the antiseptic over the splinter.

"There, now. That wasn't too bad, was it?"

The girl sniffled. "I guess not."

Well, at least the sobbing had subsided.

Rena reached into the medicine cabinet and grabbed the tweezers. Pouring peroxide over the tool, she said, "Wow. You'd think *they* were the ones with the splinters!"

Rosie looked from Linda to Kent to Grant, then back to Rena. "I'm not a baby. You can't distract me that easy. I want to watch."

From the corner of her eye, Rena saw

Grant shift his weight from one foot to the other.

"So how did you get the splinter, Rosie-girl?"

"From the apple tree. Didn't you *see* me up there? I climbed halfway up before…" Eyes wide, she studied Rena's face. "Hey, it's out already." She grinned. "Good job, Mom!" One hand in the air, she waited for Rena to high-five her.

Using a second washcloth, Rena gently washed her daughter's hand, then drizzled a few more drops of peroxide over the wound. A little antibiotic ointment and a Hello Kitty bandage, and Rosie was good as knew. "Now, let me kiss that boo-boo, and you can go outside and play."

"I'm not a baby," she repeated, standing. "Are you coming?"

Rena began putting things back where they belonged. "In a little while," she said with a smile, "but stay out of the apple tree for now, okay?"

Rosie ran outside, followed closely by her grandparents.

As Rena carried the soiled washcloths to

the laundry room, Grant fell into step beside her. "You're unflappable," he said. "Didn't know what to do, seeing her all panic-stricken. Guess the sages were right."

"About?"

"About the magic of a mother's love."

Magic, indeed. She may have pulled off *unflappable* on the outside, but inside, she'd been a shaky mess. "Her reaction worried me. Definitely something to run past Dr. Danes."

"Yeah. Maybe," he said, following her back to the kitchen. "So much for her being in a funk. The kid seems right as rain now."

"Maybe." She was tempted to press the issue, but this was hardly the time to delve into the reasons Rosie had overreacted.

"Is the grill ready?"

"Should be." He grabbed the plates of hot dogs and burgers, and shouldered his way onto the deck. "These will be ready in fifteen minutes. Need more time than that?"

Her mom stood at the door. "Never fear, Grant, Rena has everything well in hand, *as usual*. We'll be ready when you are."

Either he didn't pick up on her mother's tone, or he chose not to react to it.

"Rena is a dynamo," he agreed. "I spend half my life in awe of her talents."

When he winked at her, Rena's pulse pounded.

"I'll get started setting the table," Linda said, as Rena returned to the fridge for the salads and condiments. "And by the way, you're not seriously thinking about ordering pizza later. Your father and I will be up all night with heartburn!"

Rena repeated what she'd told Grant earlier. "Maybe you can help me make homemade cocoa."

Moments later, as they stood side by side, distributing plates and flatware, her mother leaned in close.

"Are you all right, honey?"

"Of course I am."

"Oh. Right. I forgot. We're supposed to have our talk later, after everyone else has gone to bed."

Rena was definitely not looking forward to it.

"I'm *starving* to death!" Rosie said, running onto the deck. "When do we eat?"

"Starving!" Grant echoed. "You ate a huge breakfast. And brownies!" He mussed her bangs. "Everything will be ready in a few minutes. How about if you go inside and wash up."

She held up her thumb. "But my bandage! If it gets wet, it'll fall off!"

"Then your mom will get you another one." He looked at Rena. "We have more, right?"

"A whole box."

"But…is it Hello Kitty, like this one?"

"Exactly like that one."

"Good." With that, she raced inside, letting the screen door bang shut behind her.

"See? She's fine," Grant said.

Rena's parents exchanged an inquiring look. And Grant winked at her. Again. Rena went back in to get the drinks, relieved to have something to do.

Because right now, it seemed that Rosie was the only one of them *not* acting strangely.

CHAPTER TWELVE

TINA AND LINDA took turns pushing their grandkids on the swings. Grant and Rena's siblings and their spouses, sipping iced tea and lemonade, chatted quietly on the deck. The awkwardness with Rena's parents earlier in the weekend seemed to have passed, and Grant was enjoying seeing them all together. He'd forgotten just how good it could feel.

Kent stepped up beside him at the grill.

"You never want to mash them like that. Squeezes out all the juice."

Nothing like a backseat griller, Grant thought. He grabbed the long-handled tongs and moved the hot dogs to the top rack.

"Mind if I ask you a sorta personal question?"

"Depends on the question, I guess."

"How are things going? Between you and my girl, I mean."

Rena had continued to sleep in the master bedroom since the night they'd returned home with Rosie. Did she draw as much comfort from it as he did? Or was she still just going through the motions for their daughter's sake? "Don't worry," she'd said, hours before they arrived, when he'd asked what her parents knew about their arrangement. "I've kept things vague. I don't want to rehash all the reasons we split up in the first place, and why we aren't really…well… *together* now."

He didn't want to rehash any of that, either—at least, not with the Reynolds. Truthfully, though, he hoped the sleeping arrangements wouldn't be temporary. Grant had missed the companionship aspect of their marriage as much as the romantic side.

It had surprised him, hearing that she hadn't given them a blow-by-blow of the things he'd said and done to prompt the separation.

He closed the grill's lid. "Why do you ask, Kent?"

The man's gaze traveled into the yard, where Rosie and her cousins squealed happily. "Oh, nothing in particular. Rena looks fine, but…" He shrugged. "It's like she has something on her mind. Something big."

"I'm sure she does." Grant downed a gulp of iced tea. "Getting Rosie back was big. Real big. And she's on a mission to clear every closet and drawer of unused items. The charity truck will be here any day to pick the stuff up, so she has this self-imposed deadline to meet."

"Ah-ha."

Kent wasn't buying it, and frankly, Grant couldn't blame him. For the most part, Rena behaved like the woman he'd married, easygoing and happy. Once in a while, though, he caught her staring absentmindedly into space, looking sad and lost and…lonely. One day, he'd muster the courage to ask her about that. For now, he preferred to leave things as they were. Why risk hearing that she missed her cottage at the beach, or wished they hadn't decided to share the master bedroom?

"So I take it Rosie's doctor thinks she's doing well?"

"She has a ways to go yet, but he's pleased with her progress." Grant closed the barbecue and took another gulp of his iced tea.

"Does she say much about…the past few years?"

"Not really. Trivial stuff like which books the woman read to her, how she baked cookies every weekend. At least we know there were a few normal moments." Grant rattled the ice in his glass. "The doctor says to be patient, not to rush her into talking about things, that she'll talk when she's ready."

Kent harrumphed. "That's the craziest thing I ever heard. Get it out in the open, I say, and deal with it."

"That's what I said. Rena agrees with Danes, that we should let nature take its course." He frowned at the drink. "Who am I to argue? I don't have a wig-picking degree."

Kent shrugged. "Seems to me, though, that you should have more control over things. You're Rosie's father. And I'm sure this Danes guy is charging top dollar to spout his so-called expert opinion."

"I have no problem with his fees. It's the

lack of headway that's driving *me* nuts. Every week, it's the same old thing—'Be patient. Things will happen in their own good time. Don't rock the boat.'"

"But Rosie seems well-adjusted and happy, for the most part," Kent mused.

"'Seems' and 'is'…long distance between 'em."

Kent shook his head. "I can't begin to imagine what all this has been like for you and Rena. In your shoes…"

His voice trailed off, and he stood quietly, watching his grandchildren romp in the yard. "In your shoes," he continued, "I'd want to ring that woman's neck." He started down the steps leading into the yard. "Better check those hot dogs, son."

The back door opened, startling him. Rena stepped up beside him and placed a pot of baked beans on the side burner to the right of the grill then stacked two plates on the stainless prep counter on the left side.

"One for the hot dogs," she said, "one for the hamburgers."

Grant made note of her guarded smile. "You've always been great at anticipating the needs of others." And it was true. Rena was generous to a fault, and honest as the day was long. If she had to choose between her own needs and someone else's, she'd take a back seat.

He hadn't intended to stare, but found it hard not to. She looked lovely, cheeks flushed from the day's warmth and excitement about the family get-together. Eyes wide and unblinking, she took two deliberate steps away from him.

"I'll be right back with cheese slices." A nervous laugh punctuated the announcement. "And I have to bring out the potato salad and coleslaw."

What was going on with her? Grant didn't like seeing Rena uncomfortable. Especially not in her own home. *Especially* when his behavior was no doubt part of the reason. He thought he'd been hospitable.

He'd ask her, but he'd have to wait until the family left to get into it with Rena. Between now and then, Grant intended to find a way to let her know he wanted her here, and not just because of Rosie. Every time those old memories rose up, reminding him how she'd looked the other way, he clamped down on them, hard. He hadn't allowed himself to consider the possibility that what happened at the zoo could just as easily have happened to him at the grocery store or the library. But lately, watching her with their daughter...

He followed her gaze, to where Rosie, her cousins and grandparents batted a pink ball back and forth. From the corner of his eye, though, he could see every inch of Rena, from the pale yellow sundress to her strappy white sandals. A thick braid hung over one shoulder, just as it had the first day of their honeymoon, when they'd taken an early-morning walk on Ocean City's boardwalk.

That day, Rena had stopped dead in her tracks and kicked off her shoes, eyes on the waves that gently lapped the shore. Sandal straps dangling from her fingertips, she'd raced down the rough-hewn wooden steps, facing him when her feet hit the sand. "Let's hunt for seashells!" she'd said. When he'd pointed out that she had nothing to carry them in, she'd grabbed his hand and kissed each fingertip. "That's why God gave you big, strong hands!" she'd whispered, right before planting a kiss on his lips. And even now, remembering it, Grant's pulse quickened.

Rena had been so fun and flirty, a playful and passionate partner...until Rosie went missing.

That wasn't entirely true. She'd grieved their girl's disappearance, but made a conscious effort not to appear sad—which he knew had been solely for his benefit. He'd often heard her, sobbing when she thought no one was around.

All of a sudden, he realized she'd been staring at him as if he'd grown a third eye. How much of the beautiful memory of Ocean City—or the darker one, of her lonely sobs—had shown on his face? Grant cleared his throat and faced the grill. "Need a hand carrying anything else outside?"

"I, um, I just need to grab the ice bucket and the lemonade..."

Why the hesitation? Had she been remembering the past, too?

With that, she let the screen door drift shut behind her.

Facing the yard, he hollered, "Hey, you guys! Get washed up. We're eating in five minutes!"

Every family member hustled toward the deck.

Kent and Rosie held hands. "Thank goodness," Rena's father said, "My stomach has been grumbling for an hour."

"Mine, too," Rosie chimed in before making a mad dash inside.

Linda hung back.

"Everything okay?" Grant asked her.

"I heard some of the kids asking Rosie what it was like. Being kidnapped. Living with a stranger. Being kept from you and Rena for so long…"

Grant's heart lurched. He hadn't thought to prepare her for something like that. Hopefully, Rena—being Rena—had anticipated that need and filled it. It was another thing he'd need to talk to her about later.

"What did Rosie say?"

"She changed the subject. Each and every time. It threw the kids off, and they stopped asking questions. But I saw her face. She looked so confused. And like…like it hurt to remember what happened." Linda stamped one foot. "I declare, if that woman wasn't already dead…"

"I hear ya. Rena and I feel the same way."

Linda looked over her shoulder and, assured that everyone else was still inside, said, "It's just… It's easy to see that Rosie is going to be all right." She bit her lower lip, something Rena did, too, when put on the spot. "I realize she has a long way to go, but…" She bit her lip again. "It's Rena I'm worried about. She seems fine on the surface, but I can't help but wonder how you're both handling the reconciliation."

"We're doing fine."

"I only ask because I want Rena to be happy. She's been so *un*happy for so long."

"She'll be fine. And having Rosie back is a big part of that."

Linda didn't look convinced. "I hope you're right. I want both of you, and Rosie, to be happy."

Grant pretended to busy himself adjusting the plates on the table.

"I want you to know that Rena did her best to put on a good show in the past couple

years. Of moving on and accepting things—
Rosie's disappearance and the separation."

Grant only nodded. It would have surprised him to hear Rena had cried on their
shoulders. She was the strongest person he
knew.

"But she couldn't fool us. She was miserable."

Any minute now, the family would gather
around the table.

"Speaking of Rena, I wonder if she needs
a hand with anything," Grant said awk-
wardly.

Just then, she stepped onto the deck, carrying the lemonade pitcher and tumblers on
a napkin-covered tray.

Relieved, Grant took the tray from her.
"Let me get that for you, angel."

It was what he'd always called her, prac-
tically since they'd met. It must have been
longer than he realized since he'd used the
term of endearment. Why else had her
mouth formed a perfect O as she blinked
and averted her eyes?

Dinner chatter was companionable, due
in large part to the kids' nonstop questions.

Why did people's hair turn gray when they became grandparents? What explained old people's need for reading glasses? How had Rena learned to make lemonade? And his favorite, from Rosie: Who taught Grant to sizzle up the burgers without burning them, like her other mother always did?

At the mention of Barbara, the family all but went silent. He saw the way Linda immediately looked at Rena. And the way she smiled and said, "Practice makes perfect, Rosie. Dad burned a burger or two before he mastered the grill."

Gotta hand it to her, Grant thought as Rena added a dollop of potato salad to her plate and, smiling serenely, topped it off with a few shakes of pepper.

"What's for dessert?" her brother's youngest boy wanted to know.

"Chocolate cake and two kinds of pie… apple and cherry," Rena told Tim.

"We never had dessert at my other mother's house."

Again, an uncomfortable silence blanketed the table.

"It won't go to waste with this horde!"

Grant said, breaking the ice. He speared a hot dog roll. "Besides, I love pie for breakfast. A little milk in the bowl, a minute in the microwave... Mmm-mmm-mmm. If there's any left, that is."

"Milk on pie... I remember that!" Rosie said. "'Member when I used to sit on your lap and you'd share it with me?"

The memory—and Rosie's willingness to share—touched Grant.

"How could I forget?" He gave her a gentle elbow poke. "You hogged up everything but the crust!"

Her catsup grin widened. "Oh, yeah. I did, didn't I?" Giggling, she said, "Sorry."

Linda, seated to Rosie's right, leaned closer. "When do you start school, pretty girl?"

Rosie looked to Rena for an answer.

"We have an appointment Monday morning, to meet the principal and the guidance counselor."

"Not her teacher?"

"First, we need to find out which class she'll be in. She was homeschooled at...

Barbara's. So they'll need to test her, since there are no records."

"Lucky duck," Grant's nephew, Billy, said. "You could do your schoolwork in your PJs if you wanted to. Bet you didn't have homework, either."

Rosie's smile vanished. "I never did schoolwork in my pajamas, and I had at least an hour of homework every night. On weekends, even."

Grant's sister Anni aimed a stern glare at her son, who shrugged and took another bite of his cheeseburger.

"My other mother said I was doing sixth and seventh grade work," Rosie continued. "She said kids in public school don't know half what I do."

"Why do you keep calling her your other mother?" Billy asked. "Aunt Rena is your mother. Your *only* mother."

"Now, now, Billy," Tina said, "how about we see what the rest of your cousins are doing in the sandbox?" She held a hand out to him, extended one to Rosie, too. "Want to come with us, sweetie? "

Rosie sent a grateful smile her grandmother's way and shook her head. They hadn't gone ten feet before her eyes glimmered with tears.

Seeing her in pain hurt Grant so much that he felt tears in his own eyes. He felt angry, too, at Billy for the ill-timed, thoughtless question. Yeah, he knew Billy was just a kid, but that didn't change the fact that he'd hurt Rosie! Grant was angry at himself, too, for not anticipating what might happen.

He looked at Rosie, doing her level best to rein in her emotions. But he saw that trembling lower lip and remembered it had always preceded a full-out sob session. If he didn't do something fast, Rosie would become the center of attention, and the only person who hated that more than his daughter was his wife.

Grant scooped her up and started walking toward the swing set.

"You owe me a ride on the see-saw. Time to pay up, kiddo."

He gave her a big squeeze before placing her on the seat. When she looked up at him through tear-spiked lashes, Grant thought his heart might explode with love.

"Thanks, Daddy," she whispered past a wavering smile. "Guess I shouldn't have called Barbara—"

Placing a forefinger over her lips, he shushed her. "Don't give it another thought. All you need to know is that Mom and I love you." He winked. "And that you're in for one heckuva ride, so hold on tight!"

The instant his weight lifted her up, Rosie began giggling. He wanted this for her all the time. Because his girl deserved all the joy and ease life had to offer.

He made the decision then and there to help Rosie open up—about everything. Help her deal with the past so it would no longer be a forbidden, scary place. Would Rena agree? Or would she remind him that Dr. Danes had advised against it?

Lighten up, VanMeter. She's doing her best.

But what if her best wasn't good enough… for Rosie?

He'd been tough on Rena after the kidnapping, and hadn't let up until she felt she had no choice but to leave him.

But the truth was, she'd had a choice.

And so had he.

And for Rosie's sake, they needed to acknowledge it.

THE FAMILY GATHERED in the driveway, exchanging goodbye hugs and promises to get together again soon.

"I'm so sorry, Rena," Grant's sister said, "for everything Billy said. I don't know what got into him!"

"No harm done."

"I hope you're right."

"He's just a kid, and I'm sure he's as confused about the whole situation as we are."

Another thing to love about Rena: she hated seeing anyone uncomfortable and always gave the benefit of the doubt.

Once everyone left, Grant took Rosie's hand. "Hey, kiddo, what's up? You feelin' okay?"

"I'm fine."

But she wasn't. She'd been so jovial, so spirited before Billy blurted out his untimely questions. Grant couldn't lay full blame at the boy's feet—it was natural for kids to be curious. If he and Rena had talked to

Rosie first, tried to help her prepare for such questions, they could have spared her today's upset.

"Did you get a chance to tell Grandma and Grandpa those knock-knock jokes you were practicing the other day?"

She smiled. But only a little. "Yeah, they laughed. Grandpa even told me some."

What's going on in her little head?

Rena sat with them. "I had a feeling a second dessert was a mistake," she said, grinning as Rosie picked at her slice of pie.

"I'm sleepy," Rosie said eventually. "May I take a shower and get into my pajamas?"

"Of course," Rena said, rising. "Let me get everything ready for you."

She met Rena's eyes, studied her face for a moment before saying, "I'm not a baby."

"I know that. I just love doing things for you."

Rosie inhaled a deep breath, released it slowly. "Is there time to watch a movie before bed? Even though Grandma and Grandpa went to bed?"

"Sure. Why not," Grant said. She'd had a

long, busy day, and it wasn't likely she'd last until the credits rolled, anyway.

Once she was out of earshot, Grant said, "You were right, Rena. She's fragile. The splinter the other day, and now this. Doesn't say much, but she's thinking, always thinking."

"Maybe it's time that we stopped walking on eggshells around her," Rena suggested. "And maybe, if she has something on her mind, it should come out."

Grant could hardly believe his ears. "Well, that's an about-face if ever I heard one."

"Not really. It's the way I've felt from the start." She grimaced. "But Dr. Danes is the expert, and I'm the one who messed things up in the first place, so…"

"Don't talk that way. Danes doesn't know everything. And he doesn't know Rosie. We're her parents. We're with her every day. I say we wait for the next opening and jump through it with both feet."

"I'm willing to try."

"Just so I'm clear, you agree? That we should get her to open up about—"

"About everything." Rena's eyes gleamed

with determination. "Including her feelings about me."

You mean her feelings *about how you stood by and let the kidnapping happen?*

That wasn't fair, and Grant knew it. Just because he felt that way, it didn't mean Rosie did, too. He needed to take stock, make sure he didn't let onto his own feelings when Rosie was around. Luckily, the harsh thoughts came less often these days. His fury had diminished, too. Grant didn't know how he felt about that. Playing the blame game was what had kept him strong, saved him from calling her during those lonely, hurtful months they'd spent apart. As long as he could lay guilt for the kidnapping at Rena's feet…

"Your dad asked if I thought we'd have more kids. Said something about a sister or brother helping Rosie adjust."

She paled. "You're joking."

The question had surprised him, too. Now that Rosie was back, Grant had no idea how he felt about another child. Six months or so after their girl disappeared, Rena had brought up the idea of having a second baby.

Each time, he'd said no. How did she feel about that now?

"That's terrible. I'm so sorry he put you in that position."

"He's worried about you. So's your mom. I suppose it's a fair question, all things considered."

Rena shook her head. "Still, it's way too soon to even think about a step that big. Rosie isn't out of the woods yet. And you and I…"

"We've had a lot to contend with. But as long as we stay focused on what's best for Rosie, I think we'll be okay." Even in his own ears, the words sounded hollow, half true at best.

As much as they'd diminished—and Grant worked hard to suppress them—the accusations were always there, prickling at the edge of his consciousness. Those same feelings had motivated his gritty accusations years ago, literally sending Rena packing. He couldn't afford to give in to them again, no matter how justified they might seem on the surface.

"Tomorrow, I'll have a talk with Mom and

Dad, make sure they know things are…that things are working so far."

"No need for that. I get it. They love you and Rosie and want what's best for both of you. In their place, I would have behaved the same way."

Footsteps on the stairs cut their conversation short.

"I'm finished," Rosie announced.

She looked so cute, standing there in bare feet, hair hanging in damp ringlets beside her face, the pink of her ruffle-hemmed nightgown reflecting onto her freckled cheeks. He wanted to scoop her up and hug her.

And so he did. Grant opened his mouth to tell her how much he loved her, how glad he was to have her home again, but before he got it out, she said, "Can we watch a movie now?"

Grant glanced at Rena to see if she still thought it was a good idea.

Her slow, sad smile took him back to those first days after Rosie had been taken, when his own pain and misery had prevented him from offering any consolation to Rena.

"Why don't you to pick one while I make some popcorn and hot chocolate?"

"More food! No way!"

But Rosie didn't agree. "You can't see a movie without popcorn. Besides, if you're full, you don't have to eat any."

"When you're right, you're right. But if you get a bellyache, don't come bellyachin' to me!"

Rosie followed him into the family room, where nothing but the island separated them from Rena.

Once Rosie settled beside him, Grant leaned close and whispered, "She's doing her best to be a good mom, you know."

One tiny shoulder went up, then down. "I guess."

"And it won't hurt you to be a little nicer to her."

Her expression said, *Yes, it will!* She turned away, staring through the French doors, where the porch light illuminated the deck, fading as it spilled onto the lawn. Suddenly she perked up. "Look, Dad! Fireflies!"

Rena said, "There must be hundreds out

there! When I was a kid, I loved catching them and watching them blink."

"How'd you do it?" Rosie asked.

"Grandma poked holes in a jar lid," she said, "and I collected a dozen or so and put them inside."

"Can we do that? I'll help with the holes!"

Rena took an old-fashioned can opener out of the utensil drawer. "This thing is sharp. And rusty. So it wouldn't be safe. Right?"

Rosie nodded and joined her in the kitchen. "Can I go out in my pajamas?"

"I don't see why not. But you'll need to put on your slippers. Then we'll find a jar."

The girl dashed toward the steps, slowing only when Rena added, "Grab your robe while you're upstairs. Just in case it's chilly out there."

She sent Grant an impish grin. "Okay, Mom. And thanks."

Grant winked. His message had gotten through, loud and clear. This time, anyway.

"Now, how do I tell her she's too young to stay up late enough to watch a movie after catching fireflies?" Rena asked.

"Don't worry. She'll understand. Because we'll tell her together."

Rosie skipped into the room a few moments later, pink robe flapping behind her like a superhero cape.

"Are the jars still in the cabinet under the china closet?"

Rena laughed quietly. "I can't believe you remember that's where I keep them!"

"I wasn't a baby when Barbara took me, Mom. I was *three*. I remember a lot of stuff."

Grant wondered if Rena was thinking the same thing he was: that Rosie remembered the trip to the petting zoo, too...

"Maybe one day," Rena said softly, "you'll tell Dad and me all about the things you remember."

Rosie shrugged. "Yeah. Maybe."

Grant would have sworn he heard another emotional door slam closed. And then Rosie said, "When I was with... When I was in Chicago, you were in a lot of my memories."

Rena pressed a palm to her chest. Again, Grant believed he knew what she was thinking, because he was thinking it, too: *I hope they were mostly happy memories...*

"Let's get that jar," Rena said.

Rosie ran ahead of her and began rummaging in the cabinet. "How's this one?" she asked, holding up what had been a jelly glass.

"Perfect."

"I'll pound some air holes in the lid," Grant offered.

They joined him at the counter, watching as he placed the lid on the wooden cutting board and used the can opener to pierce the metal.

"You guys go ahead. I'll be right there."

But when he stepped outside, only Rosie was in the backyard. They caught half a dozen fireflies together, and still no Rena.

"I'm going to see what's keeping your mom. You okay all by yourself?"

"I won't be by myself. There are thousands of fireflies out here with me!"

He found her in the dining room, crouched in front of the china closet. Its open doors exposed two shelves, one that held bread baskets and stacks of linen napkins, another that housed multicolored vases and an assortment of Mason jars. Kneeling beside her, he placed a hand on her back.

"You okay?"

"No. I'll probably never be okay again. Not after what I did." She paused. "Or, more accurately, what I didn't do."

"Rena. Hon. Don't do this to yourself. All that's in the past. Ancient history."

"Why shouldn't I? She remembers things, Grant. *She remembers.*" Her eyes sparkled with unshed tears. "How long before the psychological and emotional damage I've done rears its ugly head? She'll probably be scarred for life because of me!"

During the years Rosie was gone, Grant had had similar thoughts. Right here, right now? He wished he could take back every ugly thing he'd said to her. He'd meant it when he told his father-in-law that he cared about Rena and wanted only good things for her.

"Our girl's home now, safe and sound. And we're gonna get through this. Together."

She gripped his forearm with a strength that belied her size. "Be honest with me, Grant. Do you think when she finally lets it all out, she'll hate me? Do you think she hates me now?"

He had no way of knowing what damage Rosie might suffer while dealing with the truth about her past. But he couldn't stand seeing Rena this way, afraid and uncertain about the future.

"No. I don't think she hates you, and I don't think she ever will. She's a tough little girl. Think about all she survived and overcame." Lifting Rena's chin on a bent forefinger, he forced her to meet his eyes. "She's made of sturdy stuff, just like her mother."

Eyes closed, Rena turned from his touch, pretended that tidying the jars was the reason.

"That was a sweet thing to say." On her feet again, Rena added, "I know you only said it to make me feel better." A small, slanted smile brightened her face. "Thanks, Grant."

Together, they went back outside, where Rosie was giggling as she plucked the glowing bugs from the air.

"I haven't seen her this happy since she got home," he said quietly.

"I hope it lasts." Rena tilted her head toward the inky sky and whispered, "Please let it last."

"Look, Dad! Thirteen of 'em already!"

"Way to go, Rosie-girl. Way to go!"

"If you guys help, we could have twenty. Thirty, even!" And then she yawned.

"Let's see if we can get to twenty," Rena said, moving closer to Rosie. "We want to leave some for tomorrow night, and the night after that."

Nodding, Rosie dropped another bug into its new home. "Guess this means no movie tonight, huh?"

"We'll have plenty of movie nights, sweetie."

She thought about that for a minute, then said, "Yeah, I guess," and grabbed for another firefly.

"What will we feed 'em, Dad?"

"These are adults. At this age, they don't really need to eat, but when they do, they're a little like butterflies, and hang around flowers for the nectar."

"I'll put some grass in with them, to give them a soft place to sleep."

With that, she ran into the yard, eager to provide the bugs with a comfy bed. For the moment, life at the VanMeter household seemed like any other. *Hope it lasts*, he thought, echoing Rena's prayer. *Please, let it last.*

After Rosie had spent another ten minutes pushing the greens into the jar, Rena said, "We should let those fireflies go and head inside, sweetie. It's getting late."

Rosie frowned. "Can't I bring them inside with me? They can be my nightlight."

Rena and Grant exchanged a look.

Grant wanted to say yes to her, but he knew that being captured, even by tiny, gentle hands, then deposited into a glass prison, spelled certain death for the fireflies. He imagined Rosie waking up to find them lying still in the jar, drained of the light that had brought her so much joy tonight. He had to protect her from that. "The problem is they're not getting enough air," he told her.

"But…but you punched a lot of holes in the lid."

"True, but the jar is slippery, and they

have a hard time climbing up the sides to reach the lid, where their air supply is."

She stared at her captives for a moment. "If I put it on its side…?"

"Well, that'll make it a little easier for them to breathe…" He needed to try a different tack. "The thing is, fireflies don't have a very long life expectancy. They'll only live a few more days." Fewer, if she kept them in the jar. But he didn't want her to know that.

Rosie's frown deepened. She was too young to look so concerned—about bugs or anything else.

"That isn't fair," she said.

"That's just nature for ya, Rosie-girl."

"But a bunch of grass in a jar isn't nature," Rosie said. She turned to Rena. "They're going to die if I keep them in here, aren't they, Mom?"

Rena hesitated before saying, "Eventually, yes."

Rosie unscrewed the jar's lid and, stepping onto the lush lawn, gave it a shake, liberating every bug. "They should be in their real home," she said, as she watched them take flight. "It wouldn't be right to keep them for myself."

Grant swallowed against a surge of emotion. Pride in his little girl for coming to that conclusion all on her own. Anger and sadness for what had been done to her when she'd been as helpless as a bug in a jar.

Rena went to her, took her hand. "C'mon, sweetie. Let's get your teeth brushed so you can go to bed."

After placing the empty jar on the kitchen counter, Rosie looked at Grant. "Are you coming up, too, to hear my prayers?"

"Wouldn't miss it for the world."

Once Rosie fell asleep, he'd ask Rena what she thought about that moment, if she, too, suspected that the captured fireflies had reminded Rosie of what Barbara had done. If setting them free would help her heal…or if letting her capture them in the first place had done more harm than good.

Yes, he had a lot to discuss with Rena. If she didn't go into hiding the way she had been the past couple of nights…

CHAPTER THIRTEEN

AN HOUR HAD passed when Grant joined her at the kitchen table.

"What're you working on there?" he wanted to know.

"My to-do list for the next few days."

"Thought you finished that yesterday."

"I'm a horrible person. I only said that so my folks would go to bed last night and wouldn't feel obligated to get up at the crack of dawn to help me."

Grant laughed. She loved the vibrant, masculine sound of it and wished he'd laugh more often, the way he had before…

"You're not a horrible person. I was relieved when they went upstairs, too."

She drew a little heart in the margin of her notepad, colored it in and added ruffles to its edges, searching her mind for something she'd forgotten to add to the list.

"If you're finished now, can we talk?"

Rena tensed and put down her pen. "Sure."

"Did Rosie seem…different earlier? When she was asking all those questions about the life expectancy of fireflies, I mean."

"Yes, now that you mention it, she did seem preoccupied by it. I thought at the time that maybe she was identifying with them, trapped in a jar. Maybe that's how she felt after Barbara took her…trapped in that woman's house, trapped in a life she didn't want."

One brow rose on his forehead. "Whew. That's deep. That never occurred to me, but y'know, that might explain things."

"Like her bedtime prayer? I nearly cried."

Rena replayed the scene in her mind: Rosie, eyes shut tight, tiny hands folded against her chest, asking God to bless her grandparents and parents, *"…and the fireflies, too, because they're very pretty and when they light up, they make people happy."* She'd paused long enough to make Rena and Grant think her next word would be Amen. Instead, Rosie had added one last line: *"I'm sorry I caught them. Dad says*

*they don't live very long, so making them
spend any time in the jar wasn't very nice.
I promise never ever to do it, ever again."*

"She's some kid, all right," Grant said.

"I don't deserve her." Instantly, Rena re-
gretted the words. She considered self-pity
one of the most useless human emotions
and hated that she'd surrendered to it. How
often had she gone down that road? Wondering how life could have been if Rosie hadn't
been taken. She and Grant would never have
separated. And who knows? They might
have another child by now if…

"That's nonsense. You're a good mother.
One dumb mistake doesn't change that."

He hadn't always felt this way, and she
had the mental scars to prove it.

But Rena had to admit, from the moment
she'd pulled into the driveway that first evening, he'd been doing his best to make her
feel welcome. The fact that she didn't was
on her.

Grant stifled a yawn. "Don't know about
you, but the idea of hitting the hay sounds
mighty inviting."

She was tired, too, and climbing into bed did sound good.

Standing, Rena turned on the light above the stove. "Just in case Rosie wants a drink of water or something."

"I saw you do that on her first night here, and thought it was a good idea then, too."

"Do you think she tiptoes down here alone at night?"

Grant gave her a half smile. "Nah. One thing that hasn't changed…she still sleeps like a rock."

Side by side, they entered the hall and climbed the stairs.

"Watch the third step from the top," Grant said. "It squeaks loud enough to wake the dead."

Funny, but in the weeks since she'd come home, Rena hadn't noticed that.

"If you put your weight near the railing, it doesn't make a sound."

Spoken like a man who'd spent a lot of time alone in this house, she thought. Although why he'd found it necessary to maintain quiet, she couldn't say.

"Thanks. I'll keep that in mind."

She stood at the sink nearest the master bathroom door to brush her teeth.

"Cute," he said, using his toothbrush as a pointer. "I don't remember seeing those PJs before."

Rena had almost forgotten about the ruffle-hemmed shorts and matching sleeveless top, and thought it best not to mention that she'd bought them the day before he called to tell her they'd found Rosie.

He met her eyes in the mirror. "I've always liked you in that color."

"That's the main reason half my clothes are coral."

He stopped brushing. "Really?"

Did he know how adorable he looked, mouth all foamy and hair askew?

"Really."

Rena didn't know what to make of his slanting grin, but she recognized the gleam in those blue eyes.

"Do you think Mom and Dad were comfortable on that mattress?"

"I've never slept on it. But it cost a small fortune, so they should have been." Again,

Grant met her eyes in the mirror. "You don't like it?"

She'd slept in the guest room for months before leaving for Fenwick Island. "It's fine. Good, actually. It's just that with Dad's back issues and Mom's bad knees..."

Their knuckles grazed when they hung their toothbrushes in the ceramic holder.

"Your hands are cold as ice."

And his were warm, so warm she yearned to have them wrapped around hers.

"Guess it's true what they say...cold hands, warm heart."

Now really. How did he expect her to react to that? Was it a prelude to an invitation to stay in the master bedroom? *Good grief, I hope not!* She wasn't ready for that step. And considering all they'd gone through—together and apart—she didn't think Grant was, either.

Grant padded into the bedroom and she heard the rustle of covers, the telltale squeal when he climbed into bed.

"You did a great job today."

Rena leaned into the vanity and, eyes closed, said, "Yeah, the salads were pretty good if I do say so, myself. And you cooked the burgers and dogs to perfection."

"I'm not talking about the food. You were great with the family. With Rosie, too. *Especially* with Rosie."

She stepped into the doorway. "Yeah, well, you were the one who offered up all the scientific data about lightning bugs."

Moonlight slanted through the blinds, providing just enough light for her to see his slow, easy smile.

"I had no idea adult fireflies didn't need food."

He rolled onto his back. Fingers linked behind his head, he closed his eyes. She'd always loved his profile, strong and manly and wholly handsome. It seemed unfair that nature had graced him with long, lush eyelashes when it took three strokes of a mascara wand for her to get the same effect.

With no warning, he tossed the covers aside and got out of bed, crossed the room toward the bathroom. As he stood near her, Grant swallowed, and the adorable dimple appeared in his cheek. Once upon a time, she'd teased him by pressing her finger to it…right before kissing the spot. Rena resisted the urge to do it now.

He took a half step forward. "G'night, Rena," he sighed into her ear.

And then he kissed her. Not the kind of slow, searching, passionate kiss he'd treated her to before the kidnapping, but a sweet, chaste peck that left her wanting more. So much more.

For an instant, Rena thought he might kiss her again. But he turned and quickly made his way back to the bed. "Don't stay up too late. You put in a long, hard day."

Had he considered asking her to stay here, in what had been their room, instead of returning to the guest room? And if he had, what stopped him?

His steady breaths told her he'd fallen asleep. "Sweet dreams," she whispered. Almost as an afterthought, Rena added, "I love you, Grant."

"Love you, too," he murmured.

Talking in his sleep? Or had he meant it?

Hands trembling, she turned out the bathroom light.

Well, a gal can dream…

CHAPTER FOURTEEN

A WEEK LATER, the family gathered again at the VanMeters'. With all the lively conversation and jovial laughter, Rena couldn't help but feel happy.

Her brother Jake leaned around his two kids. "Pass the corn on the cob, will ya, Grant?"

Rena watched as the platter made its way down the table, growing lighter, ear by ear, as it made its way to her oldest sibling.

Her younger brother Stan, sitting directly across from Jake, raised a hand like a boy in school. "Can we get some butter down here?"

Today, thanks to the threat of rain, they'd gathered around the dining room table. Long before the family's arrival, she and Grant had stood at opposite ends, tugging to make room for two polished leaves. After putting the card table at one end and scrounging chairs from every room, they'd managed to accommodate all fourteen family members. And despite the elbow-to-elbow seating arrangement, she hadn't heard a word of complaint.

When the meal ended, Tina and Linda decided to take advantage of a break in the weather to take their grandkids—seven between them—to the playground at Sentinal Park. Grant's sisters and Jake's wife, Emma, volunteered to help clean up. Rena had never thought of her kitchen as small…until four women squeezed into it at the same time.

Grant's oldest sister took it upon herself to scrape the plates. "I've been dying to get you alone," Anni said, bending over the trash can. "How are you guys doing? No need to sugarcoat things."

"There's no need to sugarcoat anything," Rena assured her. "We're fine. All three of us."

One by one, each woman voiced her concerns. And one by one, Rena gave them upbeat, positive replies.

"If you think we're being nosy," Tressia,

the youngest sister, said, "just tell us to butt out."

"You aren't being nosy. You love us—and we love all of you, too—so it's natural that you're a little apprehensive about the situation here since Rosie came home." She met their eyes, each in turn. "You'll just have to take me at my word—we're doing all right."

Tressia rinsed a plate and put it into the dishwasher. "Has Rosie said anything about the woman who took her?"

"Nothing important," Rena said. They didn't need to hear about the numerous "other mother" references since the last barbecue.

"Are you guys thinking of private school?"

"I have an appointment tomorrow, as a Sentinal."

"Oh, I hear all sorts of good things about that school," Tressia said. "It's one of the top elementary schools in Maryland."

Rena's brother's wife tucked a handful of spoons and forks into the machine. "Next time the bunch of us gets together," Emma said, "you should use paper plates and plastic utensils."

"And deprive myself of this traditional women-in-the-kitchen scene?" Rena laughed. "No way!"

"This is nice, isn't it," Anni said. "Reminds me of Sunday dinners at Grandma VanMeter's house. The men would turn on the TV and the kids went out to play while the women did the dishes."

"Yeah. Right. Great times. The men sat around like kings while their women behaved like servants," Tressia put in. "Those were good times, all right!"

The women laughed, and Rena was relieved by the change of topic.

"What about you and Zach and Jake?" Emma asked her. "I don't remember Jake talking much about big get-togethers at the grandparents'."

"There's a good reason for that. Our grandparents all died young, so there really wasn't any place to go." Putting away the kettle she'd just dried, Rena said, "I think that's why I love it so much when everyone is here at the same time."

"Grant loves it, too," Anni added. "He

told me years ago that nobody puts on a spread like you do."

It felt good, hearing that he'd shared flattering things about her with his family. Memory of his sleepy *"I love you"* flashed in her brain, and she blinked it away.

"Your mom looks good," Tressia said. "I'd love to know her anti-aging secret!"

"Your mom looks good, too," Emma pointed out. "Every time I see Tina, I'm tempted to ask what sort of facial cream she uses!"

Even if she'd had something to contribute, Rena would have remained silent. Better that than say something that might turn their attention back to how well she and Grant were getting along since her return from Fenwick Island, or Rosie's adjustment to being home.

Tressia closed the dishwasher. "So tell me, Rena, did you own your place on Eastern Shore?"

"No, I rented a small cottage. The woman next door owned it." She needed to give Lilly a call, see how many bushels of vegetables her garden had produced so far this season.

"Bet it was adorable." Anni smiled. "You have such a knack for decorating."

"Jake told me once that when you started college, you wanted to be an interior designer," Emma said. "And that your folks talked you into courses that promised a more stable career."

"True. And the same sort of pressure is why Grant decided to go into finance." She sent Anni and Tressia a conspiratorial grin. "You knew he wanted to become an oceanographer, right?"

"No, I didn't!" Anni put a hand on her hip. "Now, how did he hide that from us?"

"He told me that after watching *Jaws* a couple dozen times, he wanted to be Matt Hooper."

"Not Quint?" Tressia put in.

"Nope, it was Dr. Hooper all the way."

"Well," Anni observed, "if he was shorter…"

Tressia laughed. "And wore little round glasses…"

"You guys!" Emma said, joining their laughter. "Grant doesn't look anything like…what's-his-name!"

Rena agreed. The actor was good-looking enough in a cute sort of way. But Grant? She sighed. Tall and broad-shouldered, Grant was downright handsome.

"Look at those dreamy eyes," Anni said. "I'll bet a dollar she's thinking about that gorgeous brother of ours."

Her sister-in-law sidled up to her. "So are things back to normal between you two, you know, the private man-and-wife stuff?"

"Emma! What a question!"

Rena only smiled, and Anni's fingers formed the universal okay sign. "In other words, things are going swell."

"Swell," Rena echoed, feigning annoyance. "Have you been watching sixties' beach movies again?"

Anni's husband entered the kitchen. "Hey, what's going in here?"

"We're talking about our husbands…"

Hands up like a man under arrest, he flattened himself against the wall. "It's getting late, and the alarm buzzes early. We were just wondering when you guys will serve dessert."

Anni pointed at the desserts lined up on

the counter and handed him a knife. "Plates are in that cabinet, forks are in this drawer."

Andy rolled his eyes and Rena gave him a gentle shove. "Get back out there. We'll pretend it's 1960 and serve you. Girls," she said, facing the women, "I believe you'll find some poufy aprons in the buffet…"

"Ha ha. Real funny," Andy said, backing out of the room.

When he was gone, Tressia glanced at the clock. "I hate to admit it, but he's right. We should pass out dessert and hit the road."

It had been a great day, filled with laughter and hugs, rousing family fun and good food. She loved these people. Loved spending time with them. Why, then, couldn't she wait until they were all gone?

Because they'd asked too many questions, questions that made her feel that they were judging her—for leaving Grant, for losing Rosie, for not having the answers they wanted.

"I'll bring the plates out," Emma said. "Will one of you grab some forks and napkins?" She pulled Rena aside and lowered her voice. "When do you think the grandmothers will get back with the kids? We need to leave soon, too."

"I'd text Mom, but…" She pointed at the counter beside the toaster, where her mother had put her phone after breakfast. First thing in the morning, she'd need to search every room, looking for her mother's wallet or pill container. Maybe she'd ask Rosie to help. Before Barbara came between them, she and Rena had been quite the team. Gardening, baking, shopping. Inseparable. How long before they regained that closeness? Would they *ever* get it back?

"Don't look so sad, Rena. Rosie will come around. You'll see."

It surprised her, hearing that her feelings were so evident on her face.

"I'm…I'm *not* sad."

Emma's caring expression told Rena that her sister-in-law didn't believe it. And no wonder, when she'd all but shouted the retort. How long after arriving home would Emma and Jake start talking about his pitiful sister and her pathetic mess of a life? Ten minutes after their kids were tucked in? Less?

"Okay then, see you in a few."

A peek out the window a few minutes later confirmed Rena's suspicions: Emma, lips mere inches from Jake's ear, no doubt telling him that things weren't picture-perfect in the VanMeter household.

If she didn't get outside, and fast, her brother would be the next one to inquire about her reunion with Grant, offering assurances that with time and patience, everything would return to normal. Just because the platitudes would be well-intentioned wouldn't make them any easier to tolerate.

FROM THE CORNER of his eye, Grant saw a flash of movement near the shed. Something small, and black-and-white. He made his way to the back of the lot to check things out, hoping as he got closer that it wasn't a skunk.

"Hey, dude," Jake said, "wait up."

Slowing his pace, he waited for Rena's brother. Just minutes ago, Jake's worried-looking wife had whispered into his ear. Grant didn't know what might have happened in the kitchen to inspire the brief exchange, but he had a feeling he was about to find out.

"Where are you headed?" Jake asked.

"Saw something duck under the shed."

"Probably a chipmunk. I saw one earlier, taking a leisurely hike on your woodpile."

Grant didn't bother saying he'd never seen a black-and-white chipmunk, especially not one the size of a small dog.

"So what's up, Jake?"

"Up?"

"I saw you and Emma earlier, acting like you were swapping state secrets."

Jake shrugged. "Emma seems to think something's on Rena's mind. She was wondering if you two are…well…if you haven't quite worked things out. Yet." Jake shrugged. "Rena's my sister, Grant. I want to see her *happy*. So if there's something I can do to help—"

"Whoa. Jake. Trust me. Things are fine. Rena is fine. Rosie's fine. I'm fine. We're all fine."

He'd grown weary of defending their situation to her family members. Hopefully, his latest speech would put an end to these examinations.

"You're sure? Because you should know, I've always liked you, Grant. I didn't take sides when Rena left."

"Meaning…you know why she moved out?"

"She never put it in so many words, but we figured it was because of what happened to Rosie. I'm guessing after a couple months of her moping around, blaming herself, you'd had your fill of it. Told her enough is enough. Deal with things. Get on with life." Extending both hands, palms up, Jake shrugged. "And knowing Rena, she didn't like hearing that, so she left."

Jake had known the girl she'd been. If he really knew the woman she'd become, Jake would realize Rena didn't give up easily. That she'd done everything humanly possible to hold things together, despite his shameful behavior.

Admittedly, Rosie had been at the heart of their disputes. But if he'd handled things like a man, Rena would have stayed.

"You're right. I *am* the reason she left. But

not because I was sick of her attitude. Because I caused it."

Jake looked mildly surprised. "Well. But. Okay. So maybe you said a few things you shouldn't have. But who'd blame you? Sounds cold, but let's face facts. She wasn't the only one suffering. What happened affected the entire family. No one more than you."

Playing devil's advocate, are you, brother-in-law?

"Not to discount what she went through or anything." Jake put his hands in his pockets. "I know you won't tell her I said all that. She already has enough on her shoulders without thinking her own brother turned on her."

In his attempt to prove he hadn't taken sides against Grant, Jake had painted himself into a corner. Grant felt a little sorry for the guy. "Mum's the word."

Jake nodded toward the house. "That cake looked pretty good. Think I'll grab a slice before Emma decides it's time to get the kids home and into the tub."

Rena's homemade chocolate cake with buttercream frosting. Knowing how much

Grant liked the recipe, she'd always made it to celebrate his birthdays, promotions, their anniversary and every time he signed a new client to the investment firm. All of a sudden, though he'd wolfed down two burgers, a hot dog and sides, Grant wanted a piece of that cake.

"Must be a big adjustment," Jake said as they neared the deck.

"What's that?"

"Well, you were a bachelor for all intents and purposes, for what, three years?"

Five years since the kidnapping, three and a half years since the separation, Grant thought. *But who's counting?*

Jake used his chin to point at Rena. "And now you're a full-time husband again. With a nine-year-old kid. A lot has changed, y'know?"

"Not that much." Rena was still his wife and Rosie would always be his little girl. Jake was right, but Grant saw no purpose in admitting it.

Jake's eyes narrowed. "So you never gave a thought to divorce? Starting over?"

"Not really."

"Yeah? Then how do you explain that all-legs blonde I saw you with a year or so ago?"

He could only think of one woman who fit that description. "That was Eileen. She's a partner at the firm. Married, with three kids. Trust me, that lunch was strictly business."

Grant looked up, saw Linda eying her eldest son. Had she sensed trouble? She'd predicted Zach and Carla's divorce long before they announced the bad news.

"I think your mom has something to tell you."

Jake groaned and hung his head. "Sheesh. Help me think of something to explain what we were talking about."

He slung an arm over Jake's shoulder and walked him toward the deck. "Sorry, pal, you're on your own this time."

Hours later, with the family gone, he and Rena headed upstairs. Hair piled atop her head in a high ponytail, she'd donned a knee-length white cotton nightie and white socks. Another woman might look frumpy in a getup like that. Not Rena.

"I think I'll read until I get sleepy," she said, dropping onto the big chair beside the bed. "Unless the light will glare onto the TV screen."

"It won't." He leaned closer to get a better look at the book. "I heard that has a pretty intense storyline," he said, reading the title. "You're not worried it'll give you bad dreams?"

Rena's gaze slid from his hand to his face. "It's a novel."

"And?"

"I've never had any trouble separating fact from fiction."

There was a look in her eyes that he hadn't seen before. Apprehension, maybe, with a tinge of anger. The women had spent a long time in the kitchen. Had she been on the receiving end of a cross-examination, too?

"Had a couple of interesting conversations lately," he began.

She placed the book on the end table and turned to face him.

"Oh?"

"With your mom and dad—separately—when they were here for the weekend. And today, with Jake."

"And these...*conversations*... Did my name come up?"

"You, m'dear, were at the heart of it all."

Eyes closed, she inhaled a deep breath. "Oh, great. Just what you needed." She met his eyes. "I'm sorry."

"For what?"

"For everything that led up to today."

Meaning if she hadn't lost Rosie, they'd never have split up, and the reunion—with all the questions it aroused—wouldn't have been necessary.

"Times like these, I wish you were more self-centered."

"What!"

"No, seriously. Hear me out." Grant scooted closer. "If you thought more about yourself and less about everybody else, you wouldn't be so quick to take the blame for... for *every*thing."

She bit her lip.

"You aren't, you know," he continued. "To blame for everything, I mean."

"True. I can't be held responsible for today's humidity. The country's political climate isn't my fault, either..."

"Be serious, okay? I'm trying to apologize here."

"*You?* For what!"

He didn't quite know how to take that. Had she meant to imply that apologies weren't in his nature?

"I'm sorry, Rena. For all the ugly things I said. For every unfair accusation."

"So you can be a hothead. So what. I've never been one of those people who does something stupid then looks for ways to blame others for it. I hope I'll never be one of those people. I'm fully aware of what I did, of what it cost all of us."

"Hon, I meant it when I said it's ancient history. How many times do you need to hear that?"

Lips and eyes narrowed, she said, "Until you can honestly say you forgive me."

Grant had half expected her to apologize for dredging up the topic that made him so uncomfortable. For making him echo those tired old reassurances, yet again. But he hadn't expected her to say *that*.

The quiet tick of the mantel clock reverberated in the otherwise silent room.

She'd never asked anything of him. Not when they were newlyweds, struggling to make ends meet. Not when her friends showed off big houses and new cars. Not when his job demanded late hours and put the household chores on her shoulders. Not even when lengthy business trips left her solely responsible for Rosie's care.

Rena had asked him to honestly forgive her. But he'd done that. Hadn't he?

The clock counted off another minute.

If he'd said it, she wouldn't have asked him to repeat it.

Grant leaned into the sofa's cushions and stared at the ceiling. How hard would it be to say those words? Say them so she believed he meant it? Because he did mean it.

Didn't he?

Somehow, he had to find a way to clear his head of that call from Detective Campbell, telling him that his three-year-old child had been abducted while her mother stood not five feet away. That, he decided, had always been the sticking point. No matter what else he told himself, Grant's mind always zeroed in on the cop's rough voice, telling him what no parent wanted to hear.

Rena hadn't heard those words. She'd *been* there in the thick of it. And when he showed up on the scene, and she ran to him for comfort…

Grant grimaced, remembering how he'd held her at arm's length. If the place hadn't been crawling with cops, TV cameras and spectators, he might have let her have it with both barrels.

He grimaced again, because despite telling himself, over and over, that she'd been a good wife and a terrific mother, that had taken a back seat to his belief that if she'd been on the ball that day…

She deserved the truth. She'd *earned* the truth. But he had some work to do first—on his attitude and the reasons for it—before he could deliver.

Another minute clicked by.

"Rena…" Grant managed to get her name past his lips, but nothing more. Maybe at some point between the kidnapping and now, he'd lost his mind. How else was he to explain that he loved this woman more than life itself, yet couldn't give her the only thing she'd ever asked of him.

"It's all right. I understand."

It was the same sweet, tender voice that had soothed Rosie when she woke with a bad dream.

"Don't torture yourself," she added.

She'd turned her head, no doubt hoping to keep him from seeing the tears shimmering in her big eyes. Rena had been so strong and brave, even during those first hours after Rosie went missing. She'd held it together because he couldn't. Only when the house was dark and she thought he was asleep had she released her pent-up heartache, night after night. Grant didn't think he'd ever heard grief like that, so raw and deep that her sobs, muffled by the pillow, shook the bed. As her sorrow poured out, he'd lain stiff and silent on his own side of the mattress, so lost in his own misery that he couldn't bring himself to comfort her.

Grant squeezed his eyes shut and clenched his jaw. If only he could put aside all the bad feelings to do right by her.

Rena got up and sat beside him, and it

wasn't until she gently wiped the tears from his cheeks that he realized he was crying. She wrapped her arms around him and began to rock to and fro. "It's all right," she said. "It's okay. You're fine. *We're* fine."

Burrowing his face into the crook of her neck, he inhaled the soft scent of her skin. "I...I'm glad you're here."

How pathetic was he, Grant asked himself, that he could say anything except *"I forgive you."*

CHAPTER FIFTEEN

AFTER AN HOUR of tossing and turning, Grant decided to get up. He slipped into the shirt he'd hung on the bedpost earlier and padded downstairs.

In the kitchen, he debated whether to have a piece of cake or a slice of pie. Neither seemed the smart choice, especially since he wasn't the least bit hungry.

So he opened the back door, wincing when it released its usual high-pitched squeal. Tomorrow, after he got home from work, he'd take care of that. For now, he chose to let it stand ajar rather than risk waking Rena or Rosie by shutting it all the way.

The sticky July air had cooled considerably since the family left. The deck chairs glistened with dew, so he leaned into the railing and stared into the yard. A cloud slid in front of the moon, leaving just enough light to cast shadows on the precise rows he'd mowed into the lawn that morning. *"Looks like the field at Camden Yards,"* Rena had said when he finished.

The grass was cool and damp under his bare feet, and made quiet hissing sounds as he made his way deeper into the yard. He needed to take care where he walked, because Zach had brought Barney, his German shepherd pup to the get-together. He'd promised to clean up the dog's droppings, but Zach being Zach, he'd probably overlooked a few. And wouldn't that just top off the night.

Should've grabbed the flashlight on your way out, he thought. Not only to look for Barney's leavings, but to zero in on whatever had ducked under the shed earlier. As he neared the back fence, the aroma of Rena's roses grew stronger. His mom was a die-hard member of the garden club, but not even she tolerated the pricks and scratches of caring for roses the way Rena did. She had endless patience with the plants, spritzing them with special chemicals to prevent black spot and kill aphids. He'd done his best to preserve them while she was gone, but his heart just hadn't been in it. Three of the eighteen shrubs she'd so lovingly planted had died. Rena hadn't said anything about it, but Grant knew she'd noticed.

The tree frogs quieted as he drew closer to the big oak, and the owl that made its home in the white pines behind the shed stopped hooting. "Sorry to disturb you, guys, but don't worry. I won't be out here long."

What exactly was he doing, standing in the middle of his yard at two in the morning, wearing nothing but boxers and a button-down shirt talking to the wildlife?

A mosquito buzzed his head. He waved it away and turned, made his way back to the deck and lit a couple of the citronella candles Rena had positioned on the tables. Surrounded now by the acrid scent, he felt an immediate calm.

Until something furry brushed his bare leg. He'd been in the Marines long enough to stop himself from jumping up or flinching. Grant looked down into the green-eyed face of a calico cat.

"Hey, girl," he said, extending a finger.

The cat sniffed it, then sat on its haunches, satisfied, for the moment at least, to look at him.

"I say girl, 'cause I hear only one percent of calicos are males."

Squinting, the cat loosed a prickly meow.

"Laryngitis?"

Silence. And then it licked its lips.

"Hungry?"

Another peculiar meow.

"If you don't mind leftovers, I've got a burger inside just waiting to be eaten."

He could almost hear his mom, warning him never to feed a stray. *"You'll never get rid of it,"* she'd probably say. *"Besides, it's probably riddled with fleas and ticks. God only knows what you might catch from the scraggly beast."*

When Grant returned to the deck, he half expected the cat to be gone. But there it sat, exactly where it had been when he went inside. He pinched a bean-sized chunk from the patty and, dropping it into his upturned palm, held it near the cat's face. When the burger was gone, he straightened and wiped his hand on his boxers.

"So," Grant said, "*mi jardin es su jardin*?"
Again, silence.

"I take it you don't speak Spanish. Allow me to translate—'My yard is your yard.'"

The cat licked its lips again.

"Thirsty?"

More silence.

Grant went back inside and came out carrying a small bowl of water. Mere moments of quiet slurping and the bowl was empty.

He made himself comfortable in the nearest chair, propped an ankle on a knee. Even in the dim glow of the candles, he noticed the cat's matted fur. A chunk missing from one ear. What appeared to be a slow-healing wound on her right foreleg. And a distinct crook in the tip of its tail. Still, clean and brushed, she was probably a decent-looking animal. Tomorrow, if she was still hanging around, he'd find a box and transport her to the vet's office on Route 108. Howard County boasted a no-kill shelter. Once the poor thing had a bath—and whatever else the vet saw fit—he'd bring it there. It was the least he could do.

Yawning, Grant stood. "Sorry, cat, but six

a.m. comes early. Feel free to cozy up under the shed. There's a bale of hay under there, left over from my seeding frenzy last fall. But you probably already know that."

As if she'd understood every word, the cat made her way toward the shed, stopping a few yards from the deck to glance over its shoulder. Something about her lost, lonely, tentative look reminded him of Rena…

He closed the door behind him, grimacing again at the ear-piercing squeal, then locked up and tiptoed through the family room on his way to bed.

"Couldn't sleep?" Rena asked from her seat on the family room sofa.

"What're you doing up?"

"I'll blame the chocolate cake so close to bedtime."

Grant sat on the edge of the cushion farthest from hers. "Maybe that's my problem, too. It's weird… I'm exhausted but not the least bit sleepy." He looked over at her. "I don't remember feeling this way after other family gatherings."

"We're older now." She smiled. "We have limitations."

The air conditioner kicked in, and as cool air pumped out of the vent above his head, Grant shivered. He could warm up in no time if he moved closer to Rena...

"Rosie and I need to be at the school by two. If you can, why not meet us there?"

Grant mulled that over for a minute and decided that if he couldn't say "I forgive you" the least he could do was show some faith in her.

"I've got a new client coming in," he said, "so I doubt I can get away in time. But you can handle things with the principal and guidance counselor. You can tell me all about it over supper."

She only nodded. Then, after a while, Rena said, "What were you doing outside?"

Grant shook his head. "Darn that squeak. I've been meaning to oil that door for months. Tomorrow, it gets done." He raised a hand, as if taking an oath. "For sure."

"Did the fresh air help calm you?"

"Not even a little."

Her soft laughter warmed him. Not as much as snuggling close to her might, but it would do. For now. He'd never loved small talk, but tonight, it felt right. Comfortable.

He considered telling her about the cat, but thought better of it. No sense worrying her about a possibly diseased animal infecting their girl. On the other hand…

"One last thing, and then I'm gonna head upstairs."

"Okay," she said, drawing out the word.

"I was talking to Joe the other day…" The older man lived on the other side of Tina's house.

"How's he doing since his bypass? I haven't seen him in the yard."

"He seemed fine. Back to fishing and puttering in his vegetable garden. But anyway, he said something about feral cats living at the back of his lot. Thought we oughta keep an eye out, make sure Rosie knows not to touch them."

"Good idea. We wouldn't want her coming down with cat scratch fever or anything."

"Definitely not. Well, g'night, Rena."

"Sleep well."

"You coming upstairs soon?"

She held up the book she'd been reading. "One more chapter…"

"Okay then. See you in the morning."

WHILE THE GUIDANCE counselor gave Rosie a tour of the school, the principal sat behind her desk, listening intently as Rena spelled out the reasons why her daughter had neither a student transcript nor an immunization record.

"We do know that she was homeschooled," Rena offered. "Rosie hasn't shared much else about her time in Chicago, though."

"I can't even imagine what you and your husband have been through these past few years. Rosie, too," Mrs. Kingston said. "My heart just aches for your family."

Rena didn't want the woman's pity. She only needed the promise that her daughter would be well taken care of here at Sentinal.

Kingston scribbled something on a notepad. "I'm sure you've already scheduled a doctor's visit to see which shots she may have been given and which she might need. While you see to those details, we'll take care of testing to see which grade level will be most comfortable for her." She picked up the pen again and used the capped end to shove her eyeglasses higher on her nose. "Speaking of doctors, I presume Rosie's seeing a therapist?"

"Yes. Dr. Danes. Once a week. The visits will continue until he feels she doesn't need them anymore."

Kingston added that to her list. "Good to know. If you'll leave me his contact information, I'll pass it to Ms. Gilmore, just in case she needs to discuss anything with him. I'll be honest with you, Rena—we've never dealt with a situation like Rosie's before. But as long as we all work as a team, I see no reason to expect problems."

Rena nodded. She only hoped the principal was right.

Kingston slid a crisp new file folder from the cabinet behind her. She printed *VanMeter, Rosalie* on its tab then tucked in the documents Rena had provided, along with the enrollment paperwork.

"We can give her a few tests today, if you have time, to assure proper placement."

"That'll be fine." One less thing to contend with later.

A soft knock interrupted the meeting.

"Are we disrupting anything?" asked the guidance counselor.

"Not at all. Come right in." Kingston stood and waved Ms. Gilmore and Rosie into the office. "We were just discussing the tests that will help us determine which class Rosie should be in."

"Tests?" Rosie sounded as alarmed as she looked. "Today?"

"It's no big deal, sweetie," the counselor said. "And it won't take a long time, either." She winked. "We want to make sure you get the very best teacher, you know?"

Rosie clasped and unclasped her hands. Had she spent enough time with Rena to pick up the nervous habit, or was it an inherited trait? Fortunately, they had decades to find the answer to that one.

"So what do you think of our school, Rosie?" Kingston asked.

She met the principal's eyes. "It's very nice. I like the pictures on the walls. And the way you painted the hallways such bright colors." She paused, stared at her fisted hands and added, "The floors are very clean and shiny, too, and I didn't see a single fingerprint on the silver things in the cafeteria. My other mother was very fussy about things like that."

If she was unsettled by Rosie's mention of Barbara, Kingston didn't show it.

"My, you're quite an observant girl, and very complimentary, too." Opening the top drawer of the filing cabinet beside her desk, the principal pulled forms from several folders and handed them to the counselor. "Might be best to let her fill these out in one of the empty classrooms, so she won't be distracted by the custodian or the painting crew in the halls."

Gilmore held out her hand and waited for Rosie to take it. "I'll get you settled," she said, leading her from the office, "and then I'll scour that big fridge in the cafeteria, see if I can't scare up a Rosie-sized carton of juice."

Halfway to the door, Rosie tugged her hand free and hurried to Rena's side. "Can you sit with me while I take the tests, Mom?"

Rena smiled, thrilled by the invitation. But the principal answered in her stead. "How about if we all meet up afterward," she suggested. "I want to show your mom around. I'm sure she'd love to see where you'll be spending your days."

Seemingly unfazed by the woman's smile, a cross between friendly and authoritative, Rosie held her ground.

Rena cupped her daughter's chin. "I'll be right outside the classroom door. I *promise*."

If she'd blinked, Rena never would have seen the flicker of doubt in her little girl's eyes. It hurt far more than she cared to admit, but this was the price she had to pay for looking away when Rosie had needed her most. Time and patience, she reminded herself, along with consistency, would prove her reliability. Until then, she'd just have to deal with the ache of knowing that her only child didn't trust her.

Rena gave in to a maternal urge and hugged her, kissed her cheek. "You're so smart," she said, holding her at arm's length. "I just know that when you're finished, you're going to tell me how easy those tests were!"

During her tour of the school, Rena asked the questions Rosie had posed to her over the past few weeks.

"Rosie has shown some interest in playing an instrument," she said as they walked among music stands and folding chairs. "What's the best way to find out which one she'd most enjoy?"

"Mr. Greene will evaluate her after school starts. He's great with the kids. I'm always amazed at the talent he manages to cultivate, with the band and the orchestra, and the chorus, too. You might want to send him an email and set up a time to discuss it with him. I'll send you home with a list of contact info for the teachers."

Rena nodded. "That would be great. What about sports? Do Sentinal students compete with other schools in athletic events?"

"No, but we encourage physical activity, not only through our PE program, but in rallies and races and on the playground. She'll no doubt enjoy our media and arts programs, too, but all that will be explained in the new student brochure I'll send you home with."

"Sounds good." Rena hesitated. "This might seem like a silly question, but what kind of clothes do the kids wear? Rosie didn't come home to us with many outfits."

"Oh, we don't have a lot of rules. No open-toed shoes, for obvious reasons. No hats indoors. No T-shirts that bear offensive language or pictures. Other than that, anything that's age-appropriate should be just fine."

"Good to know. Her grandmother and I— the one who lives next door—will take her shopping."

"Sounds like fun." Kingston's pace slowed as she said, "Since Rosie was homeschooled, you might want to prepare her for sitting at a desk. Waiting to be recognized before talking in class. Paying attention to her teachers despite the distraction of fifteen or twenty other kids wriggling in their seats." She stopped walking and lay a motherly hand on Rena's wrist. "I hope we haven't overwhelmed you." She gave her wrist a slight squeeze. "If you have any questions, please don't hesitate to ask."

They entered the teachers' lounge, where the principal offered Rena a cold bottle of water.

"I have a few phone calls to make," she said, "but you're welcome to wait here for Rosie to finish up."

"I'd just as soon wait outside the classroom if that's all right." Because it was what she'd promised, and Rena didn't want to let Rosie down.

"Of course. Stop by the office on your way out. I'll have everything ready and waiting for you. We'll see you in a few weeks."

Rena thanked her, then made her way back down the hall. Earlier, the principal had paused outside the fifth grade classrooms. Rosie sat in one of them, pencil poised and brow furrowed as she concentrated on a column of math problems. Now, as Rena peered through the rectangular window, Rosie seemed to sense her presence. She looked up and sent Rena a tiny grin and a wave.

Half an hour later, the door opened. The

counselor, carrying the test papers, led the way into the hall.

"You were right, Ms. Gilmore," Rosie told her. "Those tests were pretty easy!"

"And you completed them in record time!" The young woman met Rena's eyes. "I'll call you first thing tomorrow with the results."

As promised, they stopped by the office on their way to the parking lot. She'd half expected a thick packet of information, so the thin envelope was a pleasant surprise.

"Hey, Mom?" Rosie asked as she did up her seat belt.

Rena met her eyes in the rearview mirror. "Yes?"

"Will I be bringing my lunch, or buying it in the cafeteria?"

"A little of both, I expect. Maybe we'll find a menu in this envelope. You can buy on days they're serving things you like, and the rest of the time—"

"You'll pack me a lunchbox?"

"You bet."

"I've never had my own lunchbox before. Or a pencil case. Or a book bag. Or an umbrella. I'll need all those things for my first day, right?"

"And then some. I have a feeling your teacher will send home a supply list."

Rosie's brow furrowed slightly as she processed everything.

"All buckled up?"

"Yeah."

"Good girl." Rena started the car. "Tomorrow, Grandma and I will take you shopping again."

"Do I get to pick whatever I want?"

Rena glanced in the rearview again. Rosie looked every bit as incredulous as she sounded, a sign that Barbara had likely been a tough taskmaster.

"Of course! They'll be your clothes, after all. And lucky us, we're getting to the stores before the last-minute rush, so the selection should be good."

They were pulling into the driveway when Rosie said, "Mom?"

"Yes?"

"Will I have to wear dresses to school?"

"Absolutely not. I pass by the school every few days, on my way to the post office and the bank. I've seen plenty of kids getting on and off their buses. They wear jeans and sweatpants, T-shirts…" She pulled into the garage. "Hey, I have an idea. How about if tonight, after supper, you and Dad and I get on the computer and browse the internet? That'll give us an idea what to look for tomorrow."

"Okay. I like that idea." She unbuckled her seat belt and bounded from the back seat. "Will we get my school supplies tomorrow, too?"

"As many as we can. We won't have a full list until we find out which teacher you'll have, remember…"

"Oh, right." Rosie shoved open the door between the garage and the kitchen. "I wish we could go today."

"You promised to help Grandma with her birthday cake, remember?"

"Oh, right," she said again.

Bless her heart, Rena thought, *torn between disappointing her grandmother and disappointing herself.* After hanging her purse on the hook near the door, Rena opened the bottom drawer of her kitchen desk and withdrew a notepad and pen.

"How about we start a list of all the things you'll want to buy tomorrow. You can write them down while I'm getting supper started."

Hopping onto a stool, Rosie printed *Things to Buy for School* across the top, then proceeded to fill the entire page within minutes, with very little input from Rena.

Rosie looked so content sitting there, muttering as she hunched over her list. Rena added red potatoes and onions to the roasting pan, picturing Grant sitting beside their girl, suggesting additional things she might need. The happy domestic image nearly brought tears to her eyes.

"Want to hear my list again?"

"I'd love to." She sprinkled spices on the roast as Rosie recited, "Socks, underwear, sneakers, sweatshirts…" She paused, tapping the pen on her chin. "Are you going to make me wear undershirts when it gets cold out?"

"Yes, I will. Best way to stay warm is to keep your core nice and toasty."

"Yeah. That makes sense." She continued reading. "Bathing suit, sandals, a fall jacket and a winter coat, snow pants, a hat and mittens, and boots, too…" She paused again. "Do you think the stores will have cold weather stuff out yet?"

"I'm not sure. If they don't, we'll just have to go shopping again."

"That makes sense, too."

Rena wished Grant could see and hear her, making plans to fill her dresser and closet. Knowing him, he'd get teary-eyed.

The thought brought to mind what had happened last night. It had been the first time she'd seen him cry. Oh, he'd welled up from time to time: at his dad's funeral; again when his grandfather passed. If she'd expected Grant to react that way, Rena never would have brought up the whole forgiveness issue. Better to continue living without it than put him through that, ever again. Still, it felt good that he trusted her enough to open up. If only she could hold him in her arms like that every night for the rest of their lives! Without the tears, of course.

The family room clock chimed three

times. She'd promised to send Rosie to Tina's no later than 3:30.

"Would you like to take your list to Grandma's, show her all the things we're going to buy tomorrow?"

"She might get scared of it!"

"Scared?" Rena laughed. "Why?"

"Because it's going to take a long, long time to get all that stuff, and you know how fast Grandma gets tired."

"We'll walk slowly, and take plenty of breaks."

"Like…for ice cream?"

Rena hugged her from behind. "Yes. Like for ice cream." She kissed the top of Rosie's head. "Now, why don't you go upstairs and change into shorts and a T-shirt. And flip-flops. You don't want to get flour and sugar all over your pretty sundress."

Rosie hopped down from the stool and spun in a slow circle, delighting in the way the skirt billowed out. "It looks like an umbrella, doesn't it, Mom?"

"Yes, it sort of does."

"Why do they call it a sundress?"

"I suppose because we wear them in warm, sunny weather."

"Yeah, makes sense."

It seemed to Rena that a lot of things were beginning to make sense for Rosie. And their ordinary, everyday chatter gave her hope that maybe, just maybe, her little girl was beginning to trust her again.

"You'd better scoot. The sooner you get over there, the sooner you'll get the baking done."

"And the sooner I'll get a chocolate chip cookie."

"Exactly."

Rena heard the girl's footsteps, racing back and forth above the kitchen as she searched for a more casual outfit. And unless she was mistaken, Rosie was singing to herself, too.

Except for that quick mention in the principal's office, she hadn't said 'my other mother' in days, but Rena wasn't fooling herself. Dr. Danes's words echoed in her head: "*Sooner or later, everything she has repressed will surface. Could be a little at a time. Could be all at once. Get ready. It might not be pretty."*

But what if the doctor was mistaken? What if, instead of needing to vent about her former life, Rosie would rather file it away, deep in her memory, and simply accept that she was where she belonged, surrounded by people who'd love and protect her, always?

She slid the pot roast into the oven, set it to turn on in an hour. After tidying up, Rena flapped a linen cloth over the dining room table and, taking the good dishes from the china closet, arranged four place settings. Silver candlesticks completed the scene. Grant, Rosie and Tina would think it was all part of the birthday festivities. But as they talked about Rosie's new school, Grant's day at the office, tomorrow's shopping trip and the weather, Rena could smile at the truth: it was her way of celebrating the warming relationship between her and Rosie.

Rosie skipped into the room, looking adorable in sparkly pink flip-flops and a lavender shorts set. "Wow," she said, looking at the table, "is this supposed to be a surprise for Grandma?"

"Well, it *is* her birthday…"

She held a brush in one hand and purple elastic bands in the other. "Will you put braids in my hair?"

"You bet I will."

Rosie perched on the leather ottoman in the family room, and Rena knelt behind her, thrilled by what others might consider a mundane motherly duty. When she finished, she returned Rosie's brush. "I might have some purple ribbon in my sewing box. Want me to tie bows at the ends of your braids?"

"Sure. Do you still keep the basket in the laundry room, on the shelf above the washer?"

"Yes."

"Bummer. I was going to get it for you, but it's too high for me to reach." She took in a deep breath, let it out slowly and, shoulders lifted, said "Guess you'll just have to get it yourself."

"You put your brush away and I'll get the

ribbon," Rena said. "Meet you in the kitchen in two shakes of a lamb's tail."

Giggling, Rosie headed for the stairs, repeating Rena's words with each step. "Two shakes of a lamb's tail, two shakes of a lamb's tail. Silliest thing I ever heard. Two shakes of a lamb's tail."

She returned moments later with Mr. Fuzzbottom tucked under one arm. It surprised Rena, seeing Rosie with the bear during daylight hours. She and Grant had taken to calling the toy her cuddle buddy, since she fell asleep hugging it every night.

"Grandma said she made something for him," Rosie said, answering Rena's unasked question. "Probably a funny knitted hat or something."

She walked to the door with her.

"You don't have to take me over there, Mom. Grandma lives right next door. And I'm *not* a baby, remember."

"I remember." *But I can't let you out of my sight.* At least, not until she could be absolutely certain that her girl had safely made her way into Grant's mom's house.

"I'll make a deal with you. I'll stand on

the porch and watch until you get inside. Okay?"

Rosie tilted her head and thought it over. "Okay." She looked left, to the O'Briens' house, two doors down. Their kids were outside, laughing and shouting as they kicked a soccer ball back and forth.

"What are their names again?"

"Steven and Samantha."

"Wish I could play with them."

Logic told her that Rosie needed to spread her wings, test her limits and make new friends. But the idea of her going over there—maybe running out of sight as she joined in the revelry—struck fear in her heart.

"Tomorrow, maybe, when we get back from shopping."

The Citerony twins were outside, too, squealing as they beaned one another with water balloons.

"Oh, man, that looks like fun," Rosie said, smiling. "Bet it feels good, too. It's so hot out."

"I'll make another deal with you," Rena said. "Soon as I can, I'll call the kids' moms and arrange a playdate. They can all come over and swim in our pool. I'll make everybody ice-cream cones."

"Can we play with water balloons, too?"

"You bet. Now, you'd better get to Grandma's before she comes over here and takes you over there, herself."

With that, Rosie raced down the white-painted wood steps, braids bouncing as she crossed the strip of lawn that connected their yards. When she reached Tina's door, she turned and hollered "See you in a little while, Mom!"

Tina loved Rosie almost as much as she and Grant did, and knowing their girl was in good hands, Rena waved and went inside. The quiet hum of the cooling system was strangely calming. It was at least ninety outside, and humid, but the house was a comfortable seventy degrees. "The guy who invented air conditioner is a hero," Rena said to herself. It was a silly thought, but she treasured it, because she hadn't felt happier or more content in years.

She checked the roast, and pulled out the ingredients for a special dessert. Yes, they'd have the cake Tina and Rosie were baking. Chocolate chip cookies, too. But Rena loved chocolate mousse, and this meal was more for her than Grant's mom.

There wasn't time to stand around daydreaming. She needed to shower and change her clothes. That way, if Tina arrived earlier than expected, she could make her feel useful, chopping salad fixings. She'd wear the coral sheath Grant had complimented in Chicago. The shoes, too. And if she could find them in the jewelry box she'd left behind, the beautiful silver wolf earrings and matching necklace he'd given her the Christmas before Rosie disappeared.

Maybe Grant was right and things really were coming together. He was back at work, not calling every hour to check on her as he had that first week. Rosie was enrolled in school and having a grand time baking with her grandmother next door.

It had been a long time since Rena had felt this hopeful…

CHAPTER SIXTEEN

IT HADN'T BEEN EASY, rearranging his schedule, but by some minor miracle, Grant pulled it off. He hadn't been able to get home early enough to meet up with Rena and Rosie at the elementary school, but at least he'd be around to help get his mom's birthday dinner on the table.

He sat at a traffic light, remembering how Rosie had suggested shopping after their meeting at the school. Rena had gently said, "We'll go tomorrow, sweetie. Today, you promised to help Grandma with her cake." With less than a dozen words, she'd taught Rosie a valuable life lesson: when you give your word, you honor it, no matter what.

He could take a lesson from that, too: on their wedding day, he'd stood at the altar and promised to stand by Rena through sickness and health, for richer or poorer, forever. And yet the very first—and only—time their love had been put to the test, he'd failed. Failed the marriage. Failed Rena. Failed himself. If he'd been a smarter man, a better husband, he would have taken a page from her book. Rena had been committed to him from the start, fully prepared to honor her marriage vows, even amid his outbursts and accusations. Yes, she'd been the one to leave. But he hadn't given her much choice.

Rena was back now, though, and fully prepared to tough it out. It felt good, knowing Rosie had a mom who'd teach her strong values. Felt good that he had a wife who'd support *him*.

The way she'd supported him last night…

He steered his sedan onto Columbia Road, the *click-clack* of the turn signal keeping time with his heartbeats. Grant needed to thank her for putting up with his hotheaded outbursts. For loving him still, despite the awful, hateful things he'd said, things that drove her away. An apology, in his opinion, just wouldn't cut it. He needed to show her how bad he felt by treating her with love and respect, day after day, until she *believed* in him again.

Pressing the button that sent the garage door up, Grant pulled into the driveway...

...and slammed on the brakes, unable to believe his eyes.

Rosie raced around the O'Briens' lawn, purple-bowed braids bobbing. She giggled when Steven tapped her shoulder and bellowed, "Tag! You're it!"

Grant got out of the car, pocketing his keys as he walked toward them. He scanned the yard, looking for Rena. She was probably on the porch with Christine, supervising the horseplay. No way would she have let Rosie out of her sight again.

"Daddy!" Rosie yelled, throwing her arms around his waist. "You're home early!"

"Aren't you supposed to be at Grandma's?"

"I saw the kids," she said, blinking up at him. "I wanted to play."

"Where's your mother?"

"In the house, I guess."

"Does she know you're over here?" he barked.

Her happy smile vanished. His gruff tone had caused that. Grant had never raised his voice to her before. Not when she broke his college football trophy, not when she spilled milk on his suit moments before he had to leave for an important client meeting, not when she threw her ball in the living room—after he'd told her not to—and broke the window.

"I just wanted to play."

The O'Brien kids stood quiet and still, watching the entire exchange. Rosie had been home for weeks now, but between appointments, family gatherings and getting her acclimated to being with him and Rena again, there hadn't been time to introduce her to the neighbor kids. He felt like a heel for spoiling her fun. But he wouldn't have had to if Rena was here…

Grant wanted to give her the benefit of the doubt. Maybe she'd taken Rosie to his mom's, as planned. His mother had never been able to say no to this kid; if she'd asked to go outside and play…

He made a concerted effort to gentle his

voice. "What about Grandma? Does *she* know you're here?"

"No…"

The one-word reply told him Rena hadn't brought her next door. He still couldn't believe she wasn't here!

"Sorry, kids," he called over his daughter's head, "Rosie has to go home now. She'll see you later. Maybe."

Reluctantly, she accepted his offered hand. He'd deliver her to his mom's house, making sure his girl was safe, and then he'd find out *why* Rena had let Rosie out of her sight.

"Sorry, Dad. I didn't think anybody would mind." Glancing over her shoulder, she waved at Samantha and Steven. "They were having so much fun," she repeated. "I wanted to have fun, too."

"It's okay, kiddo. Nothing wrong with having fun. But from now on, you need to tell Mom or me or Grandma where you're going."

He opened his mother's front door and led Rosie into the foyer. "Mom?"

"In here, honey." Wiping flour-dusted

hands on a kitchen towel, she said "You're home early. Did someone cancel a meeting?"

"I did."

Now, his tone erased his mother's smile. Grant slapped a hand to the back of his neck. He'd hurt two of the people he cared most about, all because Rena hadn't been where she was supposed to be.

"Sorry," he said. "It's been a crazy day." Kissing Tina's cheek, Grant added, "How's the birthday cake coming?"

"Haven't started it yet." She smiled at Rosie. "I was waiting for this li'l munchkin." She bent to meet her granddaughter's eyes. "It isn't like you to be late."

"Sorry, Grandma."

"No need for that." Straightening, she added, "Do you remember how to run the electric mixer, the way I taught you last week?"

Rosie nodded.

"Well, the cake batter is ready for you. Think you can get started without me?"

"Sure, Grandma. And don't worry, I won't lift the beaters out of the bowl and make a big mess like last time."

"That's my girl." She watched Rosie climb onto the kitchen stool and adjust the beaters, then led Grant into the hall. "What's going on?"

"Rosie was at the O'Briens'. Without Rena."

Chin raised, she examined his face. "I see."

But did she? Did his mother realize how terrified he'd been, seeing his girl over there, alone and unsupervised?

"I need to get home. You and Rosie gonna be okay for a while?"

Tina snorted. "We'll be fine. And by the time we get over there with that cake, you two had better be fine, too." She punctuated the statement by jabbing a finger into his chest. "That child needs stability, not a lot of up and down, back and forth between her parents."

"But, Mom—"

"Don't 'but Mom' me. I'm sure Rena has a perfectly legitimate explanation. Before you fly off the handle and start the war of the VanMeters, give her a chance to tell you what happened." Arms folded, she added,

"Now go. Get straight with your wife. You owe her that." With that, she turned on her heel and left him standing in the hall.

He took his time crossing the lawn. When he confronted Rena, he wanted to be cool, calm and collected. Because his mother had been right: nothing could be accomplished if he stormed in there huffing and puffing like an angry bull.

The house smelled great when he stepped into the foyer. Pot roast, unless he was mistaken. His mother's favorite. His, too. He opened the fridge to grab a bottle of water, saw a row of small bowls lined up on the bottom shelf, each filled with chocolate mousse. Rena's favorite. His, too…next to chocolate cake with buttercream frosting. Grant frowned. Had she let meal prep get in the way of minding Rosie?

"Rena?" He entered the dining room, saw that she'd already set the table with the china and the good linens. The place looked like something out of a decorating magazine. She liked his mom and wanted the birthday dinner to be something special, but to go all-out like this? Grant didn't get it.

"Rena!"

"I'm up here," she called from the top of the stairs. "I'll be right down."

He didn't have to see her to know that she was smiling.

Her sandals slapped the soles of her feet as she hurried down to meet him. She was wearing that dress he liked so much. She'd put her hair up, too. A few strands had escaped the clip and now curved alluringly alongside her face. The earrings he'd given her sparkled in the sunshine. She'd put on the matching necklace. If she'd ever looked more gorgeous, he couldn't remember when. But he couldn't let that distract him.

"I'm so glad you're home early. I nearly called to tell you about our meeting at the school, but I didn't want to interrupt a meeting or anything. I think our girl is going to love—"

"Our *girl*," he interrupted, "was at the O'Briens' when I got home."

Her smile vanished, exactly as Rosie's had moments ago.

"That's impossible," she said, taking a

cautious step back. "She's with your mom. I watched her walk over there myself."

"I saw it with my own eyes. She. Was. At. The. *O'Briens'*."

Eyes wide with shock, she tucked the curls behind her ears. "But…but she opened your mom's front door. I watched her!"

"Why didn't you bring her *in*?"

"She…Rosie asked me to let her walk over by herself. Said I needed to quit treating her like a baby. I thought…I thought what better way to show her that I have confidence in her, so said okay, all right, you can walk over by yourself, but I'm going to watch you…" She bit her lower lip. Then, blinking, Rena repeated, "She opened the door. I saw her."

Why did she keep *saying* that?

"Yeah, well, she never went inside. She saw those kids goofing around in their front yard, and went over there to join in on the fun." He shrugged out of his suit jacket, hung it on the hall tree. "She's nine, Rena. *Nine*. You're her mother. You should have realized a kid her age might be tempted, especially after she came right out and told you what she wanted to play with them," Grant said, rolling up his sleeves.

Cupping her elbows, her voice shaky, she whispered "You're right." Slumping onto the bottom step, she buried her face in her hands. "Anything could have happened between here and there. A stranger might have driven by. And…and…we don't really know the O'Briens all that well. What if she went into their house and one of *them*…"

He felt bad, seeing her this way, but he had more important things to worry about than her hurt feelings. Because Rena was right: anything could have happened. He couldn't survive another abduction. He'd barely survived the last one! It wasn't just that risk, though. How could he live with himself if something *else* happened to her, mere weeks after they'd finally got their Rosie-girl back?

"I'm at a loss, Rena." He began to pace from the front door to the staircase and back again. She hadn't just let Rosie down, she'd let him down, too.

"I have responsibilities at work, clients to take care of." He stopped, looked her square in the eye. "I can't be here all day, every day, making sure you're doing your job. I *adore* that kid, Rena, and if I can't rely on you…"

"I love her, too, you know." She got to her feet. "I've been doing everything I can to help her readjust. I gave up my job, my career, to dote on the two of you. You have no right to talk to me this way, Grant. I've earned more respect than this."

She took a step closer and stared at him, hard.

"I watched her walk over there. Saw her open the door and start to go inside." Rena leaned on the newel post. "But you're right. I should have known better. The kids were out there, kicking a soccer ball around. The Citerony twins were across the street, too, throwing water balloons. Rosie asked if she could go over, but I told her no, because she'd promised to help your mother. I felt so bad, disappointing her that way when all she wanted was to play like any other girl her age. So I made a deal with her, said I'd ask the other moms if the kids could come over, swim in the pool, have ice cream and…"

She shook her head, as if still trying to wrap her mind around what he'd told her.

"It's just that Rosie is such a *good* little girl. I never would have guessed she'd just go off on her own that way. I'm sorry it happened. It won't happen again. So you can *stop* treating me like some empty-headed, errant child. You know me, Grant. You know, somewhere deep inside that stubborn heart of yours that I'd never do anything to hurt that child!"

Part of him *did* believe that. And yet…

"This isn't getting us anywhere," he said.

"Nothing like this will happen again. Not because you blew in here like a storm trooper, hurling accusations left and right, but because I love her every bit as much as you do."

He couldn't very well deny that. Every look, every word, every action proved how much Rosie meant to Rena. And when he cooled off, he'd admit it.

"Mom made a point of telling me she expected us to pull ourselves together before she and Rosie get here."

Rena responded as if she hadn't heard his last words.

"You need to stop pretending that watching her like a hawk is the answer to everything. For one thing, it's impossible. For another, you'll suffocate the poor kid. As you so astutely pointed out, she's *nine*. We need to teach her about boundaries, not stick her in some protective bubble where she never has to think or make a decision, or— God forbid—a mistake! How do you expect her to learn what her limits are if you insist on us hovering every minute of her life? Just because you don't agree with that is no reason to hate and mistrust me, Grant!"

What she'd done had scared him, but he didn't hate her for it. Rena had never lied to him. So why not give her the benefit of the doubt, now?

Then he remembered something his mom had said, about how unlike Rosie it was to be late. It told him that she and Rena had set an arrival time. Technically, she was almost as much to blame as Rena.

Almost.

He took a deep breath. "Um, need a hand with supper?"

She brushed past him, chin up and back stiff. "Except for warming the rolls, everything is ready."

"I could put ice in the glasses…"

"Believe it or not," she bit out, "I can handle it."

Interesting choice of words. After their heated exchange, Grant supposed she had every right to be angry with him.

"Listen, Mom and Rosie will be here any minute…"

"Give me a break, Grant. You know as well as I do that I'd never spoil your mother's birthday dinner. And after the wonderful day Rosie and I had, I refuse to let her see that you and I are…that we're…that we're upset with one another. So we'll table this for now, but you'd better believe we'll talk about it later!"

He'd never seen her this angry, but after the things he'd said, Grant could hardly blame her. For some reason, last night came to mind, when he'd blubbered like a schoolgirl and she'd soothed him, even though he couldn't bring himself to say "I forgive you." Why couldn't that have come to mind *before* he behaved like a belligerent bully?

Rena had said she deserved better, and she'd been right.

CHAPTER SEVENTEEN

SOMETIMES, RENA THOUGHT, sliding the rolls into the oven, living with Grant was like being trapped on a roller coaster. One moment, his behavior was cold and distant. The next, warm and loving. In those brutal months following the abduction, he'd bluntly refused to hash things out with a therapist, leaving her to accept the mood swings as his clumsy coping mechanism. How would he have reacted if their roles had been reversed, and he'd been the on-duty parent that day at the petting zoo? Not well, she told herself. Not well at all.

Until they'd had Rosie, he'd handled every crisis with his unique brand of calm strength. When gale-force winds kicked up by Hurricane Isabel ripped shingles and gutters from the roof and caused a leak that ruined an entire front corner of the house, he'd gone outside in the middle of the downpour to tack a blue tarp over the gaping hole. That time when an elderly woman squealed out of a parking space and T-boned their days-old SUV? He'd pointed out that they'd both be old someday; if they ever caused a similar accident, he hoped their victims would react with kindness and understanding.

Matters relating to Rosie, however, had always sent him careening downhill at breakneck speed: the time she came down with roseola, and her fever spiked to 103 degrees, Rena had thought he'd wear a path in the carpet, pacing until the toddler's temperature came down again. And what about the fall from the swing at the playground, when she got up screaming, arm bent at an odd angle? Then, the day Rosie tumbled from her tiny two-wheeler, skinning both knees and elbows, he'd wanted to take the bike to the Marriottsville landfill.

The ups and downs had taught Rena to hold on tight. As her dad so often said—during political campaigns, weather-related calamities, and while watching the evening news—"You gotta look at the big picture."

It made it easier to remind herself that Grant was a good and decent man, a loving husband, a doting father. That was what she told herself, over and over, during the worst period of their marriage. Easier, but not easy. Bottling it up hadn't been good for either of them. Everything she'd told him this afternoon should have been said on the night she'd left for Fenwick Island.

Well, it was out in the open now, and if he didn't drop the holier-than-thou attitude, Rena would tell him everything else she'd bottled up all these years. The things he'd said today had the power to drive a permanent wedge between them...if she allowed it. *Let's face it,* she thought, *you love him, warts and all.*

"Mom's here," he said, carrying a covered cake stand into the kitchen. "She and Rosie are going to play Old Maid while we get dinner on the table."

"Sounds like fun. You should get some pictures."

Whether he hadn't picked up on her sarcastic tone, or chose to ignore it, Rena couldn't say. But it sure felt good to stand up for herself for a change!

"I'll take pictures later, when Mom's blowing out the candles." He lifted the lid, and winced. "Coconut. Blech."

"It's her favorite. When it's *your* birthday, I'm sure she'll bake a chocolate cake."

He replaced the cover. "Need a hand with anything?"

The oven timer beeped, as if on cue. And instead of her customary, *"No thanks, I've got it,"* Rena said, "You can put those rolls into the basket over there, and bring them to the table." Maybe if they worked like a team, they'd feel more like one.

He slid open the utensil drawer and withdrew a pair of tongs. "What's the cheese for?" he asked, pointing at the bricks of cheddar, Muenster and pepper jack on the cutting board.

"It's an after-dinner snack." She slid the blade of a knife into one of the wrappers and peeled back the plastic. "A nice change from popcorn."

He tossed rolls into the napkin-lined basket. "So I've been thinking…"

"Oh, great. Lucky me."

Frowning, Grant continued with, "Thank you. For agreeing to set our disagreement aside until later, when we're alone. I know you and Mom are close, but—"

"I've never shared anything personal with her in the past, and see no reason to start now."

"Not even during your marathon phone calls while you were on the shore?"

"Especially not then."

"Hmm…"

"Don't start, Grant. It's the truth."

"But she's told me you two could spend upwards of thirty minutes gabbing."

"So?"

"What did you talk about, if not me, and what I did?"

Rena rolled her eyes. "Billions of things happen in the world every day, and most of them don't revolve around you."

He winced. "Ouch."

Really now, what did he expect? That she'd perform a happy little jig, just because he'd said thanks? She wasn't his trained seal!

"Breathe easy, Grant. Your mother will

never guess that anything is wrong between us. I'll make sure of it."

Grant stood in the arched doorway between the kitchen and dining room. "How?"

Wiggling her eyebrows, Rena pretended to hold a cigar, à la Groucho Marx. "'Cause I've got a million ways to distract her."

Shaking his head, he disappeared into the dining room. Rena had every intention of sticking to her get-tough guns, but only when Grant forced her into a corner. The rest of the time, she'd treat him with respect and kindness, just as she always had.

Because their relationship—their family—quite literally depended on it.

GRANT PUSHED BACK from the table and patted his stomach. "You outdid yourself tonight, Rena. That roast was perfection."

"He's right," Tina said. "I've never been very good with beef roasts. No matter what I do, they always turn out tough and stringy." She looked across the table at her son. "Isn't that right, hon?"

Hands up like a man held at gunpoint,

Grant said, "You've never heard me complain, have you?"

Tina sniffed. "Only because you're an advocate of the 'don't bite the hand that feeds you' theory."

True to her word, Rena had kept the conversation going all through the meal, but now quiet fell over the table. "Is everyone too full to have dessert now?" she asked, breaking the silence. "I can serve it later, once our meal has had a chance to diges—"

"Let's do it now!" Rosie bounced up and down in her seat.

Standing, Rena began clearing the table.

Tina rose, too, and gathered up a handful of silverware.

"Oh, no you don't," Rena said. "It's your birthday. I'll bring you two some decaf, and you can talk about…"

She didn't miss Grant's silent warning.

"…the weather. The news. Rosie's visit to the school." She lifted a stack of plates. "I'm sure you'll think of something."

"Can I put the candles on the cake, Mom?" Rosie asked.

"That'd be great, sweetie."

She sprinted into the kitchen, and Rena called after her, "No running in the house, Rosie. You could trip and fall!" Turning back to the table, she added, "I made chocolate mousse, if either of you would like some to go with your cake."

"I'd love some," Tina said.

RENA HOPED TINA wouldn't notice that Grant wasn't his usual jovial self.

In the kitchen, she found Rosie, precariously balanced on a stool as she tried to get the candles out of the baking supplies cabinet. Heart pounding, Rena stifled a gasp then in one swift move, swept Rosie into her arms and set her back on the floor.

"Standing on a wobbly stool isn't the best idea, sweetie. What if you fell?"

"Oh. Yeah." Shoulders raised, she grinned and, in a deliberately innocent voice, said, "Will you get the candles down for me, please?"

Rena stood on tiptoe and grasped the box. "How many should I use?"

"Let's see… How about six candles for the sixty, and another five for—"

"I get it. Good idea, Mom."

Rosie dumped the candles onto the count-ertop, and as she pressed each into the cake, Rena filled three cups with coffee. Placing them on a tray with the sugar bowl, creamer, and spoons, she said, "You did a great job, sweetie. I love the way you've spaced them out."

"Thanks." She looked up to ask, "When will I be old enough for coffee?"

Rena picked up the tray. "If you like, I'll make you a cup to sip with your breakfast tomorrow." With plenty of milk and a little sugar, the way her own mom had fixed it when she was a girl.

"Really? Cool!"

Rena had nearly reached the doorway when a scary thought stopped her.

"Soon as I deliver this, I'll come back and light the candles. You'll be in charge of turn-ing out the lights. Okay?"

"Okay, Mom."

Mom. The most beautiful word in the English language. She could hear it a thou-sand times and never tire of it.

When Rena walked into the dining room,

Tina was laughing at something Grant had said. "Here you go," she said, placing cups and saucers beside their plates. "Rosie and I will be right back with the cake."

"All finished," Rosie said when Rena returned to the kitchen. "What else can I do?"

Rena tapped a fingertip against her chin. "Hmm… Think you can get everyone a clean fork and spoon and bring them into the dining room?"

She hurried to fulfill Rena's request. "Don't bring the cake in there 'til I get back," she whispered, "so I can go first and turn off the lights."

"Okay," Rena whispered back.

As she lit the candles, Rena wondered at how near-perfect her life was. Yes, she and Grant still had a few wrinkles to iron out, but what married couple didn't? Patience and a whole lot of love would, in time, smooth things out. Maybe continuing their discussion wasn't such a great idea after all.

Rosie appeared in the doorway, hands clasped and eyes bright. "Okay, let's get this show on the road!"

Laughing, Rena picked up the cake and

followed slowly, guarding the flames with one hand. The instant she stepped into the dining room, Rosie hit the light switch and began singing the birthday song. Grant joined in, and as Rena placed the cake in front of Tina, she sang, too.

When the song ended, Tina blew out the candles and Rena handed her a serving knife.

"Make the first cut, birthday girl, so I can plate it up."

"I'll do it," Tina said. "You need to get that chocolate mousse!"

"Okay, but first, how about opening your presents?"

Rosie disappeared around the corner. A moment later, they heard the sounds of crinkling paper and a slamming door. She appeared carrying a construction paper card, a store-bought envelope, and a gaily-wrapped package that had been topped off with a little-girl-tied floppy bow.

"I made this for you," she said, handing the card to her grandmother. And as Tina read it, Rosie slid the package closer. "I made this, too."

"I love this," Tina said, closing the card. "Now, what's in here?"

She untied the satiny blue bow and peeled back gleaming silver paper, exposing a picture frame made from popsicle sticks and decorated with red pompoms. Beneath the glass, a photograph of Tina, holding baby Rosie in her lap.

"I found it in Mom's album, and she said it was okay to give it to you."

Pressing the frame to her chest, Tina smiled. "I love it. It's just beautiful."

"You can put it on your nightstand, so the last thing you see before you go to sleep is *me*!"

"You know, I was thinking the same thing!"

Now, Rosie handed her the tidy envelope. Tina pulled out a glittery card, which Rena and Grant had signed with birthday wishes, and a gift certificate to attend any production at the historic Hippodrome Theater.

"Kids, this is so generous and…and wonderful!"

"You can bring your friends," Rosie pointed out. "It's enough for three tickets!"

As she had with Rosie's picture frame, Tina held the certificate to her chest. "I love it. Thanks, all of you. I don't even mind that the other kids decided to take that cruise on the Bay!" She waggled her eyebrows at Grant then looked at Rena. "My son can be a generous guy when he wants to be, but he never would have thought of something like this all on his own. So thanks, Rena."

"We love you, Mom."

She didn't often use the title when speaking to or about Tina, but seeing the delight that lit up her mother-in-law's face, Rena was glad she'd used it just now. She looked past the candlesticks and birthday cake, coffee cups and bowls of mousse separating them, and met Grant's eyes. She couldn't get a read on his mood, but unless she was mistaken, his ire had cooled. Rena sat back, content to watch and listen to the loving interactions between him, his mom and Rosie. Their easy rapport made Rena doubly grateful for this life of hers.

It made her think of the tiny cottage on Fenwick Island, with its view of the old lighthouse. Nearly every day, she'd wondered about the lost souls led to safety by its beacon. Wondered what had become of those who hadn't seen it in time. It had helped her hold on to hope that someday, Grant would want her again.

Tomorrow, she'd call Lilly, tell her to rent the place to someone else, because thanks to Rosie, *this* lost soul had found her way home.

Things could be better, there was no denying that. But they could also be a whole lot worse. Rena had a happy child—for now, at least—and a loving family. And then there was Grant. Sure, he had faults, but none she couldn't live with. She had a few warts, herself. *And that lends balance to our relationship, right?*

Still, there was one thing Rena needed from him that she wouldn't compromise on: he had to forgive her. *Really* forgive her. Or none of this would last.

"I need more coffee," she said, standing. "Either of you want a refill?"

Tina and Grant declined.

Rosie said, "Mom's gonna let me have coffee with breakfast tomorrow!"

"Oh, she is, is she?" Grant asked.

She couldn't tell at first if he approved or not. But then he winked at their little girl and said "Well, I guess it's okay, as long as it's decaf."

Wonderful. Now she could sleep, free from fear of his disapproval.

Sarcasm, she thought, wouldn't solve any of their problems.

But it sure did feel good...once in a while.

CHAPTER EIGHTEEN

WHEN RENA INSISTED on doing the dishes herself, Grant didn't put up too much of a fight. She seemed to want her space, and he couldn't blame her.

He sat in the family room, mulling over their earlier confrontation, searching for ways to justify his behavior. After seeing Rosie at the O'Briens' and finding out that Rena didn't know she was there, he'd felt he had to do something. And he'd been right, hadn't he? How else could he ensure it wouldn't happen again?

Grant pictured the way she'd reacted to his lecture this afternoon, drawing her shoulders inward, as if trying to fold herself up and disappear. Her usually rosy-cheeked face paled, making her eyes appear twice their normal size. She'd shrunk back, not because he'd scared her, but because he'd demeaned her.

He derived no satisfaction from that. Instead, shame burned his cheeks and swirled hot in his gut. He wasn't a complete idiot. He knew all kids disobeyed their parents, that from time to time, they snuck away to romp with their friends. On the one hand, he was grateful that Rosie felt secure enough to separate from Rena; on the other, he wasn't ready for his little girl to spread her wings. He'd believed Rena's side of things, so why had he continued to lash out at her?

If he was honest, he'd needed to vent his fears and frustrations. What better target than the woman he trusted more than anyone in the world?

Then he remembered the way she'd stepped right up, hands on her hips as she gave every bit as good as she'd gotten. Hard as it had been to be the recipient of her fury, he'd never been more proud of her. Every word had been right on point, and he owed it to her to admit that sooner rather than later.

Grant toed off his shoes, left them beside the recliner and joined her in the kitchen.

Rena had already finished the dishes—no surprise there, but a disappointment, because he'd hoped to renew his offer to help out.

Grant noticed right away that she'd changed out of the pretty dress and into black, calf-length leggings and a long white T-shirt. His T-shirt, unless he was mistaken. He must have dozed off for a minute, and that was why he hadn't noticed her pass through the family room on her way upstairs.

"Sure doesn't take you long to—"

Rena whirled around and flattened a hand to her chest. "Good grief, Grant, you scared me half to death!"

"Sorry. Didn't mean to startle you."

That was when he spotted the platter of cheese cubes on the cutting board, the knife in her right hand and a bright red trickle of blood trailing from the tip of her left forefinger to her wrist.

He went to her, took the hand in his and inspected the cut. "Did I make you do that?"

"I didn't hear you come in."

So he *had* caused it. Grant hadn't thought

it possible to feel any worse about himself. He'd been wrong.

He grabbed a paper towel and stood at the sink to dampen it. "Doesn't look too deep," he said, wrapping it around the wound, "but if it doesn't stop bleeding in a few minutes, I'll call Mom, get her to stay with Rosie while I take you to the ER for stitches."

"It's fine," she said, and tried to withdraw from his grasp.

But Grant held on.

"Did I thank you for supper?"

"Sort of."

"Sort of?"

She looked up, big eyes scanning his face. To see if he had a mind to continue what he'd started this afternoon? The notion cut through him just as surely as that knife had sliced her finger. He relieved her of the blade, placed it on the cutting board and popped a cheese cube into his mouth.

"You said everything was delicious. I took that as a sort of thank-you."

"Everything *was* delicious." He grabbed another chunk of cheese and held it near her mouth. Instead of turning her head, as he'd expected, Rena parted her lips and let him feed it to her.

"Seemed like your mom had a good time," she said around the cheddar.

"She did."

"Rosie, too."

"That gift certificate was a great idea. Mom's right. I never would have thought to get her something like that."

"You put in a lot of hours at the office, and I'm here all day. Plenty of chances to chat with her. She happened to mention a few weeks ago that she hadn't been to the Hippodrome since it was remodeled."

"Hmm. That was a long time ago…"

Small talk. They both hated it, yet here they stood, doing just that. Again. They'd been communicating really well until he blew her out of the water for not being a mind reader. *You're a self-centered idiot*, he told himself. Rena loved Rosie at least as much as he did…

He peeled back the blood-soaked paper towel. "Looks like the bleeding has stopped."

"Good. I hate the ER."

Chuckling, he let go of her hand. "I'll get

you a bandage. Think you can stand the sting of peroxide?"

"I'll try and be brave."

He tossed the towel into the trash can and made his way to the powder room, found the box of Hello Kitty bandages she'd stored in the medicine cabinet, along with the antibiotic ointment and peroxide. Carrying all three to the kitchen, he thought of the last thing she'd said before he left the room: *"I'll try and be brave."*

Rena was the bravest person he'd ever met. The way she'd soldiered through those awful days right after the kidnapping, while he wrung his hands and sang woe-is-me… Yeah, he had a lot to make up for, all right.

"Here y'go," he said, depositing the first-aid supplies on the island. He pulled out a stool, patted its seat. "Take a load off, lady. I have work to do."

A faint smile lit her eyes as she did what he asked. A sign that his earlier outburst hadn't pushed her too far? *A guy can hope…*

He grabbed a dishtowel and draped it across her lap. "To catch the peroxide," he explained, unscrewing the cap. Rena winced slightly as he dribbled the liquid over the cut. After drying it with a fresh paper towel and applying some ointment, he wrapped the bandage around her finger.

"There. Almost good as new."

She looked up at him again, sending his heart into overdrive with her sweet, sad smile. He held her gaze, searching for proof in those beautiful, long-lashed eyes that they would get through this.

"Good job, Dr. VanMeter. Thank you."

"I don't work for free, you know."

Brows high on her forehead, Rena blinked. "I'm unemployed. Will you accept monthly payments?"

He cupped her chin and said, "It won't cost much." Then, gripping her upper arms, he put her on her feet. "Just this."

Still holding tight to her arms, he pulled her near and kissed her. And much to his amazement, she closed her eyes returned it. Rena went a little limp, but Grant was more than happy to steady her.

A blissful moment passed before she sighed and tipped her head back. "I should put that cheese away before it dries out."

"Let it. We'll buy more," he said, and kissed her again.

"This window faces your mother's house, don't forget…"

Grant looked up, saw the light in his mom's kitchen glowing bright into the darkness. "I think she's seen people kiss before," he said, combing her hair with his fingers. "Besides, we're married. Nothing wrong with a husband showing a little affection to his wife."

Rena let out a surprised little gasp and he picked her up, not bothering to turn off the light or check to see if the doors were locked as he carried her toward the stairs.

She didn't fight it at all. Instead, Rena rested her head against his shoulder, stroking his cheek, his forehead, his hair.

While trying to make the turn on the landing, he grunted quietly.

"Guess I shouldn't have had cake *and* mousse," she said apologetically.

"You're light as a feather. I just didn't want to wake Rosie by banging your head against the wall."

A whispery laugh escaped her lips. "Gee. Your care and concern is so touchi—"

He silenced her with yet another kiss, then eased her onto the bed. "Man, you're gorgeous in this light."

Grant didn't know what to make of that look on her face, but it gave him a flicker of hope that she didn't hate him for treating her so poorly for so long.

He lay down beside her and pulled her close.

"I'm sorry," he said. "Today, earlier…" He pressed his lips to her temple, hoping to buy enough time to regain his composure. "I got scared, is all, and wasn't thinking straight. There's no excusing the way I spoke to you."

"It's okay, Grant. I get it." She turned onto her side, lips touching his as she whispered, "Just don't let it happen again."

Her no-nonsense tone surprised him, but things were going too well between them to ask what she'd meant. Then Rena kissed him like she meant it, and Grant threw himself into the moment.

Suddenly, she stiffened and pushed away. "What's that?"

He couldn't hear anything over his own ragged breathing. "What?"

"It's Rosie. I think…I think she's crying!"

Rena was out of his arms and across the room before he could wrap his mind around her words. He followed her into the hall.

They found Rosie sitting up in bed, clutching Mr. Fuzzbottom to her chest.

"Aw, what's wrong, sweetie?" Rena sat beside her, gently stroking bangs from her forehead. "Bad dream?"

"I hate her," Rosie choked out.

Rena looked up at Grant, and in the dim glow of Rosie's nightlight, he could see that she was worried. He was, too.

"I hate her and I'm *glad* she's dead!" Rosie said, punching the mattress. "She took me away. Far, far away. We drove and drove. She *lied* to me, and when I cried because I thought you were dead, she said if you loved me, you wouldn't have been driving so fast. But there wasn't an accident. You were with me at the zoo."

Her sobs subsided as Rena held her tight, rocking and chanting, "It's all right. It's okay."

The very words she'd spoken to *him* last night. It didn't surprise Grant that her soothing tone calmed their little girl. Rena had always had that touch with Rosie. And with him. All he had to do was think about those exquisite moments with her, and whatever had upset him, *didn't* anymore.

Grant sat on Rosie's other side, pressing kisses to her tear-streaked cheeks. "Your mom's right, kiddo. You're home now. You'll always be safe here with us."

Sniffling, Rosie nodded.

"What happened to your finger?" she asked Rena.

She met his eyes over Rosie's head and, smiling, said, "Oh, I wanted some cheese and had a little dustup with a kitchen knife. It's just a tiny cut."

The girl grabbed Rena's wrist, brought the hand to her lips and kissed the bandage. "You used to do that every time I got hurt. You did it when I got the splinter, and that's when I remembered. And when I knew Barbara lied about that, too. You *did* love me, didn't you?"

"Loved you then, love you now. I'll love you my whole life."

There were tears in her voice. And truth be told, Grant felt a little choked up, himself. Rosie had just experienced an important breakthrough. But was this the end of it, or just the tip of the iceberg?

"I don't want to call her my other mother ever again. And I really *am* glad she's dead."

Rena took a deep breath and met his eyes again. Gently stroking Rosie's hair, she said, "I'm sure that's how you feel now, but Dad and I want you to know that if you ever change your mind, it's okay. Barbara did some bad things, but—"

"Some *very* bad things," Grant put in.

"—but she took pretty good care of you, made sure you had plenty to eat and a safe place to sleep. I'm grateful for that."

Nodding again, Rosie exhaled a huge sigh. "I guess. Still…"

Too soon to ask questions? Grant wondered. He tried to remember what Danes had said about that, and when nothing materialized, he said, "She never hit you, did she?"

"No."

"Never locked you in a closet or anything, right?"

"Right."

"And she didn't put rocks in your socks?"

That inspired a quiet giggle. "No."

"Then, like Mom said, if you change your mind about hating her…"

"But, Dad." She started to cry again. "I missed you guys, and it was all her fault that we couldn't be together!"

He almost said *not as much as we missed you*, but stopped. He didn't want to inadvertently make her feel guilty for the pain he and Rena had endured. Danes had cautioned them about that possibility, though Grant didn't agree with much the doctor had to say, that was one warning he'd been careful to heed since they reunited with their little girl.

"I'm so glad you guys aren't really dead."

Rena plucked a tissue from the box on the nightstand. "We're pretty happy about that, too." After gently blotting her eyes, she held it to their daughter's nose. "Blow," she said, and Rosie did.

Such a simple gesture, yet one so maternal and tender that Grant's heart thudded with love for her.

"Can I ask you a question, Mom?" She leaned into Rena's side.

"Sure, honey. Anything."

"Were you really friends with her in college?"

"No, sweetie. I'd never even heard of her until a few days before we brought you home."

"Hmpf. So she lied about that, too." She punched the mattress again. "I thought only kids told big fat lies."

"Grown-ups tell them sometimes," Grant said. He caught Rena's gaze. "And sometimes, they say really stupid things, too. Things they don't mean. Things that hurt the people they love more than anything in the world."

Rosie looked up at him. "But not you. Or Mom. Right?"

"Oh, yeah," Grant replied. "Even us."

"But only once in a while," Rena said, "and only when we're under a lot of stress."

Rosie's brow furrowed as she thought about that. "What kind of stress?"

Rena bit her lower lip, and Grant jumped in with, "The kind that happens when you're scared, or mad, or confused. Sometimes it makes you do or say things without thinking first."

"Oh." She hugged the bear a little tighter. "Are you mad at Mom?"

"No, sweetie." Grant reached past her and grasped Rena's hand. "I'm not mad at Mom." He gave her hand a little squeeze. "She might be mad at me, though."

"Really?" Rosie faced Rena. "What did he do?"

Rena's quiet laugh was as soothing as soft rain on the roof. Grant held his breath, wondering what amazing insight she'd share with their girl.

"He didn't turn off the kitchen light. Didn't lock the back door, either."

Eyes on Grant again, Rosie said, "Well?" She made a shooing motion with her free hand. "Hop to it, mister!"

"Women. You all stick together, don't you?" he teased.

On his way to the bedroom door, Grant felt relief flood through him. Rosie might have a ways to go yet, and certainly had more to reveal about her life in Chicago, but she'd be okay. *She'll really be okay!*

And Rena… He visualized the way her face had flushed earlier, the way she'd melted into his arms…

Grinning like a happy fool, he turned and clapped once. "So! Who's in the mood for popcorn and hot chocolate?"

CHAPTER NINETEEN

ROSIE WAS OUT of bed and beside him in a flash. "I'll have some!" Facing Rena, she said, "Coming, Mom?"

"In a minute. I'm a little chilly so I think I'll grab my robe."

She watched them descend the stairs, hand in hand, chatting all the way. Hard to believe that just moments ago, Rosie had sobbed and bared her soul. Part of her soul, anyway.

Rena entered the closet, reached for her white, knee-length terry robe.

Was the outburst proof that Rosie's healing process had only barely begun? Or had the crying jag cleared her system? It wasn't normal, was it, that she'd said so little about Barbara or her time in Chicago? *Of course it isn't*, she thought, slipping into the robe. She made a mental note to ask Dr. Danes about it at their next session. Or maybe, instead, she should call Martha. It had been months since they'd talked. She could bring her old therapist up to date, then ask for her professional input and spare herself looking like a nincompoop in Danes's eyes.

What would her former doctor say about the way things were going with Grant? Rena tried to see it from a psychologist's point of view: *Get some perspective, Rena. Look at the situation from all angles. Make a list of pros and cons. Good things and bad...*

She stepped into a pair of backless slippers and hurried downstairs. Upon entering the kitchen, she saw Rosie and Grant, side by side in front of the microwave, hands on knees as they watched the popcorn bag inflate. *Item number one for the pro side of the list*, she thought, smiling: *He's great with kids*.

The steady pop of kernels filled the kitchen with the scent of salt and butter, and when the timer dinged, they both straightened and shouted "It's about time!"

Item number two: *He's not afraid to act like a kid*.

"While you fill the bowls, I'll warm up some milk for the hot chocolate."

"Oooh, that's a pretty robe, Mom." Rosie turned to Grant. "Doesn't Mom look pretty?"

He shot Rena the slanted smile that had caught her eye so many years ago. "Yeah, she's pretty all right."

Was she imagining things, or did he look…*off*? "You feeling all right, Grant?"

"Yeah, why?" He drove a hand through his hair.

Rosie studied his face. "Your face is all shiny."

Grant grabbed a paper towel and blotted his forehead. "Maybe I was standing too close to the microwave."

Hands on hips, Rosie said, "Even I know that a microwave is only hot on the *inside*, Dad."

He looked at Rena, eyebrows and shoulders up. He expected her to come to his rescue, but she wasn't sure she could. For one thing, his eyes were glassy and his lips were pale.

"Have a seat," she told him, pulling out

a chair. "I'll get the hot chocolate." She grabbed a mixing bowl and dumped the popcorn into it. "There y'go. Dig in!"

He rested both elbows on the table and held his head in his hands.

"Headache?" she asked, pouring milk into a saucepan.

"The mother of all headaches. Hit me from out of the blue. Weird, because I never get headaches."

Rena pressed the back of her hand to his forehead. "You're a little warm." In fact, he was burning up, but she didn't want to alarm Rosie. She opened the cabinet beside the sink, shook two ibuprofen tablets into her palm, then grabbed a bottle of water from the fridge. "Take these," she said, "and drink that water."

"All of it?"

"Every drop."

"But I'm fine. Just tired. All I need is a good night's sleep."

Rena mixed cocoa with sugar and vanilla and stirred it into the milk. "Whipped cream on top?" she asked Rosie.

"No, just plain, please," she said around a yawn.

Well no wonder. It's 12:45.

Rena filled two mugs with the lukewarm mixture. "Drink up—it's way past your bedtime. Both of you."

A minute later, the popcorn bowl was still full and so were the mugs.

"All right, you two. Upstairs and into bed." Hands on Rosie's shoulders, she said, "You first, missy. I'll be up in a minute to tuck you in."

On the way to the door, Rosie paused. "'Night, Dad. Happy dreams, and I hope you feel better in the morning."

He sent her a weak smile. "You, too, kiddo. And don't worry. I will."

Rena waited until she heard Rosie's door click shut, then got the thermometer from the powder room medicine cabinet.

"Open," she said, holding it near Grant's mouth.

"I don't need that." He waved it away. "I told you. I'm fine."

"You're not fine. I didn't want to say anything in front of Rosie, but you have a fever. We need to see just how high it is."

"It'll be normal, you'll see."

"Uh-huh. Humor me," she said, sliding it between his lips.

"Yrre crrzy. Yrr knww thtt?" he mumbled around it.

Crazy about you... "Shh. Don't distract me. I'm timing this."

"Hww musssh lngrrr?"

"Thirty seconds. If you stop talking."

Grant tapped his fingers on the table, keeping time with the kitchen clock's second hand. "Okay, time's up," he said, handing her the thermometer.

Rena held it up to the light. "102.6." She looked at him. "You're going to bed, right now."

Even Grant couldn't argue with that number. He staggered up the stairs, and Rena followed. She threw back the quilt and fluffed his pillows.

"Thanks, Rena." He flopped onto the mattress, and as she covered him up, he grabbed her wrist. "What say we pick up where we left off?"

"Are you kidding? You have a fever!"

"Right. What was I thinking. I'm probably contagious."

"I never get sick. You know that. I'm not worried about catching what you have. It's just that you need your rest."

"No." He wrapped both arms around her. "I need *you*."

She tried to wriggle free, but he tightened his hold. "You're delirious."

Rena waited for a well-timed joke, a pun…anything. Instead, he said, "How soon before I can take more ibuprofen? My head's killing me."

"Yes, it's too soon. But I can get you a cool cloth. And more water."

She raced around to gather what he needed, and when Rena got back, he was sound asleep.

Or so she thought.

"This is Joe Michaels's fault," Grant muttered. "We sat head to head going over his file day before yesterday, and he breathed germs on me the whole time. Said his boy brought some bug home from college." He groaned again. Shivered, too. "The kid's probably as sick as I am, or I'd charge him extra percentage points instead of the going rate on his investment portfolio."

"Stop talking and go to sleep." Rena tucked the covers under his chin. "And FYI, if you still have a fever in the morning, we're going to see Dr. Stewart."

Something unintelligible passed his lips.

"I mean it. Go. To. Sleep."

"Mmm. Sleep. Love you, Rena."

She smoothed the blankets over his chest, letting her fingers linger there for a moment. "I love you, too, Grant."

His brow furrowed, even as he slept, and she blamed it on the headache. Rena gently refolded and pressed the damp washcloth to his forehead, and he exhaled a slow, relieved sigh.

She sat in the overstuffed chair beside the bed and, wrapped in a puffy comforter, watched him sleep. Hours later, a crick in her neck woke her. He'd kicked off his covers and now lay in the fetal position, quaking as if resting on a block of ice. Tossing her blanket aside, Rena went to him. "Well no wonder you're shaking like a leaf," she whispered. "You're drenched with sweat!"

She couldn't get him into dry pajamas or change the sheets without waking him. But his sleep wouldn't be restful if he was that uncomfortable, and he needed to stay hydrated. And in a few more hours, another dose of ibuprofen.

Rena nudged him awake. "I'm going to run a cool bath for you."

"No way. I'm already freezing!" he said, clutching at the covers.

"All right then. We can try cool compresses on your face, neck, back and legs. And I need to take some of these covers away."

He moaned. "If I say I'm sorry, will you promise not to torture me with cold water?"

"Sorry? For what?"

"For everything. Stuff I said. Things I did."

"Ancient history," she said. "Now try and get some sleep."

Rena turned the washcloth over, startled by how hot it felt. "I'll be right back."

He grabbed her wrist. "You're the best."

She bit back fear-induced tears and made up her mind to be cheerful for his sake. "I know."

"You'll really be right back?"

"I promise."

"And you'll never leave me again?"

"Never."

"Promise?"

His normally strong baritone sounded thready and weak, and that concerned her.

"Promise. Now go to sleep."

"I really am, you know."

"Am what?"

"Sorry."

"Me, too," Rena said.

"You? For what?"

"For not being able to figure out how to get you to go back to sleep."

A brief chuckle, then silence, followed by his soft, steady snores.

RENA WOKE TO the sound of raindrops pecking the window pane. It was still dark outside, so she levered herself up on one elbow to peer over Grant's shoulder to check the time. 4:35. And fortunately, he seemed to be sleeping peacefully.

Ever so lightly, she stroked his cheek, hoping to feel cool, whisker-stubbled skin. But it was clear his fever had spiked higher still.

As she debated whether or not to wake him and get him to take more ibuprofen, the squeaky floorboard in the hall near Rosie's room alerted her that her daughter was out of bed. Within seconds, the master bedroom door opened.

"Mom? Are you awake?" she whispered.

Rena moved back to the easy chair and patted the space beside her.

"Is Dad still sick?"

"'Fraid so. But he'll be fine. I'll make sure of it."

"Because you're a nurse?"

Because he has to be. "Something like that." She pulled the coverlet over Rosie's shoulders. "So what happened? Did you have another dream?"

She cuddled close and nodded.

"You want to talk about it?"

She nodded. "I was thinking about the day my oth...when Barbara died."

"I'll bet that was scary."

"After she fell, a nice lady came over and got onto her knees next to Barbara. She did that thing with her fingers that people do on TV shows, and touched Barbara's neck. Then she called 911 and brought me to a bench. A bunch of people were standing around saying stuff like 'Is she dead?' and 'What happened to that lady?' But they were all talking so fast that I couldn't understand anything else. I started to cry, and the nice lady said the ambulance would be there soon and I shouldn't be scared." Rosie hesitated. "But I was."

Rena pulled her closer, trying to imagine what that must have been like for Rosie, who'd had very little contact with anyone but Barbara for five years. "You're a very brave, very strong little girl. I don't know many grown-ups who could have dealt as well with a thing like that." She hugged her tighter. "I'm so, *so* proud of you."

"I'm sorry I said that I'm glad she's dead." Leaning back, she peered into Rena's face. "Would it hurt your feelings if I said I kinda miss her sometimes?"

"Of course not, sweetie." She kissed Rosie's forehead. "You spent a lot of time with Barbara, counted on her for everything. She might not have been the perfect mother, but for a long time, she was the only mother you had. You wouldn't be my sweet, big-hearted Rosie if you didn't love her."

Kids, Danes had explained, often compartmentalized the traumas and tragedies in their lives. *Call it a survival tactic or a coping mechanism,* he'd said, *which allows them to feel their lives are normal.* Because she'd been so young when the abduction took place, Danes believed that Rosie had taught herself to concentrate on the good things about Barbara rather than her more unpleasant traits.

"I'm so sorry, sweetie. So very sorry."

"Because Barbara is dead?"

If it made her a bad person, so be it—in truth, Rena couldn't be happier about that! She couldn't very well admit it to Rosie, though. "I'm sorry that she took you away from us, and I'm sorry she scared you with the story about the car wreck." There were so many more reasons to be sorry, but Rena didn't feel it was wise to share them with Rosie. Not now. Maybe not ever.

Rosie sat, quiet and still for so long that Rena thought she might have dozed off.

"Can I ask you something?"

"Of course, sweetie. Anything."

"You didn't leave the petting zoo, like Barbara said, and drive too fast and get in an accident?"

"No, I didn't."

"Then…then where *were* you?"

It was the question she'd dreaded. Rena's answer could mean the difference between a Rosie who felt safe, and a Rosie who'd have trust issues for the rest of her life. If only Grant was feeling well enough to be a part of this conversation!

"What do you remember about that day? The part before Barbara took you, I mean."

"I was petting the baby goats. Most of the other kids were, too, because they were so tiny and cute, and made funny noises."

"Do you remember Suzi?"

"Who could forget *her*? She kept getting into trouble."

"And do you remember what Suzi was

doing while you and the other kids were petting the goats?"

"She wasn't listening to the teacher. Or to
you." She paused. "Hey, wait…she almost
climbed into the pen with that huge bull.
And he was *mean*! But you scooped her up
in time."

Rena had always wondered how much of
that Rosie had seen. "Exactly. And that's
where I was—at the bull pen—and that's
what I was doing—getting Suzi out of
there—when…when Barbara…when she
took you."

She'd come right out and admitted that,
even as a kidnapper prowled among the
children, her attention had been on another
child, not her own. Rena held her breath,
waiting to hear her little girl's reaction to
the ugly fact.

"I kinda think I know why she picked
me."

"Oh?"

"I was in Barbara's room one time, looking through her jewelry box…"

Rosie had always loved standing at Rena's
dresser, trying on bracelets and rings. She'd

loved clomping around in high heels, too, and pretending to apply blush, using Rena's makeup brushes…

"I found a picture of a little girl. She had my same hair color. I asked who she was and Barbara got mad. She said it was her little girl, who died. Then she put the picture back and sent me to my room, and said if I ever touched her things again, I might get a spanking."

"I'm so sorry, sweetie. If I'd been watching you instead of Suzi…"

She hadn't meant to say that. Could have kicked herself for saying it! *"Answer the questions Rosie asks,"* Danes had warned, *"and don't press her for details. She'll tell you what she needs to, when she needs to…"*

Grant began to stir and moan.

"Let's get you back to bed so I can put cool washcloths on Dad, to bring his fever down."

"It's okay, Mom. I can tuck myself in. You take care of Dad. And I'm not mad anymore."

"Mad?"

"You don't have superpowers, so you couldn't be in two places at once."

Rena had no idea how to react to that, and so she simply told the truth: "I love you, sweetie. Love you so much!"

"You know what?"

She was almost afraid to hear.

"If Suzi had gotten into that pen, the bull could have stomped on her. And that would have been really, really awful, you know?"

"Yes, it certainly would."

"You saved her life."

Maybe, but at what cost?

"And I'm okay, so…so I guess things worked out for the best."

Was it possible that Rosie had actually come to such a conclusion all on her own? Rena leaned back to get a better look at her daughter's face. "Are you *sure* you're only nine?"

"You guys talk too much," Grant croaked out.

How long had he been awake, and how much had he heard? Rena got up and, one knee on the mattress, reached out to feel his forehead. "Oh, my goodness. You're burning up."

He tried to turn toward her but winced. "My neck is so stiff," he said.

If Rena had been worried before, now fear gripped her. She'd read an article in yesterday's paper detailing a meningitis outbreak at several area universities. What if Grant's client's son had come down with meningitis instead of a nasty cold? Then infected his dad…who had passed it on to Grant?

She faced Rosie once more. "I need to get you to Grandma's so I can take this fella to the doctor's."

"He's gonna be okay, right?"

Rena heard the fear in her little girl's voice.

"Soon as the doctor figures out what's wrong with him, he'll prescribe some medicine. And you and I will make sure he takes it!"

"Oh, great," Grant groaned. "*Two* women bossing me around."

Rosie giggled. "Da-a-d, I'm not a woman, yet!" She looked at Rena. "Want me to make him some toaster tarts to eat on the way to Dr. Stewart's office?"

"Cherry?" Grant asked.

"I think they're blueberry, Dad."

"With icing?"

"And sprinkles."

"Perfect."

Rosie hurried down the hall as Rena made her way to Grant's side of the bed.

"Man. I'm dizzy. And I ache all over."

Could it simply be the flu?

"Maybe all I need is a hot shower."

"Cool shower, you mean. Need any help getting there?"

"Nah, I should be okay. And by the way, I only asked for the toaster tarts to keep her busy. Stop her from worrying. I'm not the least bit hungry, so you're gonna hafta figure out what to do with them."

"Leave everything to me."

Grant staggered to the bathroom and turned on the water as Rena dialed the doctor's cell phone. The family practitioner had entrusted her with the number shortly after Rosie was born—being a nurse had its perks. While waiting for him to pick up she pulled sweatpants and a sweatshirt from Grant's dresser.

When the doctor picked up, she quickly explained that Grant may have been exposed to meningitis. After listing his symptoms, she pleaded with Dr. Stewart to see Grant, as soon as possible.

"Don't take him to the ER. His immune system is down and Lord knows what he could pick up. Plus, he could spread it to everyone in the waiting room. Can't say anything for sure until I get a look at him," Stewart said, "but I'll call the office as soon as we hang up, make sure we can get him in by nine."

Rena thanked him, then asked, "Can I give him more ibuprofen? He's miserable."

"No, better wait until I see him. We don't want the medication to alter the labs. We'll need to run a few tests." He paused. "But based on what you said, sounds like we'll need to transfer him over to Howard General."

"I half expected that," Rena admitted.

"See you in a few hours. In the meantime, push fluids."

Rena thanked him and hung up, then went to check on Grant.

"You all right in there?"

When he didn't answer, she slid open the door and found him shivering on the shower floor.

Rena quickly turned off the water and grabbed every towel in sight.

"Can you stand up?" she asked, draping them over his shoulders.

He scrambled to his feet. "Aw, look. I got everything wet, including you."

"We have a linen closet full of towels."

She needed to get him onto his feet and into warm, dry clothes.

"Okay, ready? Lean on me…"

"You're kidding, right? I'm a foot taller and outweigh you by sixty pounds."

"Which means you'll have to help a little. Now come on. Lean on me."

After several faltering steps, Rena got him into the bedside chair and made quick work of getting him dressed. Despite the sweats, he continued to shiver. She grabbed a fleecy jacket and slid his arms into it. He was too weak, though, to be much help. Muscle weakness, she remembered from the article, was another symptom of meningitis.

"Is the light bothering your eyes?"

"Yeah, as a matter of fact, it is."

"Fingers tingling?"

Grant flexed both hands. "A little." He frowned. "What's going on?"

"I'm not sure." But she was. "I'm going to call Dr. Stewart, have him meet us at the Howard General. You can't wait until nine o'clock."

"No way. All I need is sleep, like you said before."

"Grant, we're going to the hospital. Period. Now, you stay put while I call the doctor. And your mother. Got it?"

He sent her a crooked little smile. "Yes, ma'am."

CHAPTER TWENTY

FIFTEEN MINUTES LATER, armed with the knowledge that Rosie was safe with Tina and the doctor would meet them at the ER, Rena turned on the car's emergency flashers and drove twenty miles over the speed limit.

And Grant, the classic backseat driver, didn't even notice.

Parking at the hospital's entrance, she raced inside and grabbed the first wheelchair in sight.

"Get in," she said, opening the passenger door.

He climbed out. "I can walk in there under my own steam, Rena."

Grant had no sooner completed the sentence than he had to grab the car's roof for support.

"Get in," she said again. And this time, he complied.

"It's meningitis, isn't it."

"Could be. But Dr. Stewart said he needs to run some tests to be sure."

She rolled him toward the registration desk as he said, "I really *am* gonna double-bill that jerk, Michaels."

"Let's get you checked in first, okay?" She faced the counter and told the woman behind it, "Dr. Stewart told us to meet him here… Grant VanMeter?"

The woman checked her log. "Yes, the doctor is on his way." She buzzed for an intern, who took Grant into an exam cubicle. "You can join him," the clerk said, "just as soon as you've filled out these forms."

Rena hitched her purse strap higher on her shoulder. "That's my husband in there, and he needs me. So I'll fill out these forms once the doctor gets here. Okay?" With that, she marched past the partition and found Grant already lying on a gurney.

A nurse joined them. "I'm Marian," she said, smiling. "Dr. Stewart would like to get started right away." She placed several empty vials on a stainless-steel cart. "We'll need to get you undressed," she told Grant.

And after pulling the curtain around them, she handed Rena a blue gown. "Are you okay to help him, or do you need me to do it?"

Rena unfolded the gown, placed it beside Grant on the bed. "We'll be fine."

"Good. We need to get some fluids into him, so I'll just grab a few things and be right back."

The curtain was still billowing from her hasty departure when Grant said, "Man. They don't waste time around here, do they?"

"That's a good thing, wouldn't you say?"

Dr. Stewart joined them a few minutes later, and after snapping surgical gloves over both hands, he stepped up to the bed. A second nurse followed him, and fired up the computer that hung on the wall.

"So when did you start feeling awful?" he asked Grant.

"Late last night."

Marian returned, wrapped a tourniquet around Grant's upper arm, and inserted the IV needle as Stewart continued. "Been around anyone with cold or flu symptoms in the last week or so?"

Grant told him about Michaels and his son, and Stewart nodded as the nurse entered the data into the PC.

"And who, other than your wife, have you been in close contact with?"

"My mother, my daughter, my secretary, couple guys at the office…"

He turned to Rena. "If it turns out he has meningitis, we'll need to get in touch with all of them, so they can be tested."

Because it's highly contagious, she thought with a shiver.

Marian released the tourniquet and began filling vials with Grant's blood.

"Put a rush on those," Stewart said when she finished. "I want results within the hour."

She looked dubious. "I'm nowhere near that good at schmoozing."

He smirked. "Tell the lab techs I have a pocketful of gift cards. That oughta put Grant here, at the top of their list."

Then he helped Grant sit up, pressed a stethoscope to his back. "Deep breaths,"

Stewart said. Moving to Grant's chest, he said, "Breathe normally."

Next, he strapped on a blood pressure cuff, slid a finger pulse oximeter onto Grant's forefinger. And while the equipment buzzed and beeped, he took Grant's temperature.

The nurse, reading the screens, added the data into the computer.

"I have a couple of other patients to see," Stewart said. "Soon as they text the lab reports, I'll let you know what's next."

"Such as?" Grant asked.

"Lumbar puncture, scans…"

"How long does it take to get those results?" Rena asked.

"If the blood cultures lean toward meningitis, believe me, it'll be fast." He gave her forearm a reassuring squeeze.

"And if it turns out I do have meningitis?"

"Treatment will depend on whether it's viral or bacterial." He parted the curtain. "Don't worry. I'm on this." And with that, he disappeared.

"While we're waiting, maybe you could bring Mom up to speed," Grant suggested.

Rena agreed, and stepped into the hall to make the call. Doing her best to sound confident and unconcerned, she promised to call again when the test results came back.

"Rosie wants to talk to you," Tina said.

"Mom? Is Dad okay?"

"He's fine, sweetie. There's nothing for you to worry about."

"When will you guys be home?"

"The doctor is doing a few tests," Rena said, "so he'll know what kind of medicine to give Dad. It could take a while, because hospitals can be slow sometimes. I'll call you and Grandma as soon as I hear anything, okay?"

"Okay. And Mom?"

"What, sweetie?"

"Tell Dad I love him."

"I will."

After a long pause, she added, "I love you, too."

"And I love *you*. Could one family have anything more?"

"A baby brother or sister, maybe, or…or a *puppy*!"

"You're a little nut, you know that?"

Rosie blew kisses through the phone, and after they hung up, Rena returned to the registration counter and completed the proper paperwork. When it was done, she went back to check on Grant, who'd fallen asleep.

She slid a stiff-backed chair closer to the bed and sat beside him, watching, waiting, listening to every raspy breath. He looked cold, so she stepped into the hall and searched for a blanket warmer. Spotting one, she half ran to it and helped herself to a short stack of blankets, then hurried back to Grant.

His tight-clenched fists relaxed when she covered him.

He opened his eyes and gave her a weak smile. "Thanks, Rena. You always know just what to do."

Stewart pushed into the cubicle and announced that he'd ordered scans and a spinal tap.

"I'm fairly certain you have meningitis. And considering how fast your symptoms worsened, I'm guessing the acute bacterial variety. Someone will be here shortly to take you to the radiology department. I'm gonna sit on 'em, make sure I get the results back, fast."

"What's the rush, doc?" Grant asked.

He looked as worried as Rena felt.

"So we can get the right antibiotics going to nip this thing in the bud." Facing Rena, Stewart added, "I'll write prescriptions for you, your daughter and your mother-in-law once we're sure. Strictly a preventive measure, mind you. But I'll need some basic info about all three of you so I get the dosages right."

"I need to call home with an update, anyway. I'll have that information for you, soon. If we need the drug, when will we need to start taking it?"

"Immediately." He glanced at Grant, looked back at her. "Personal question?"

"Of course."

"When was the last time you two had marital relations?"

Rena took a step back, shocked by the question. "What does that have to do with anything!"

But she knew, even before he said, "Meningitis is transmitted through bodily fluids."

"We kissed tonight," Grant said. "Couple of times."

Stewart nodded. "We could be whistling in the dark, here." He shrugged. "Could be some other infection."

"But you don't think so."

"No, Grant, I don't think so."

A burly orderly entered and announced he was there to take Grant for tests. As he rolled past, Rena clasped his hand. "I'll be there just as soon as I've talked to your mom. And by the way? Rosie said to tell you she loves you."

His smile was as weak as his grasp. "Tell her I love her, too, and that I'll be home soon."

The farther down the hall he went, the smaller and more vulnerable he looked. *Soon*, Rena repeated. *Come home with me soon.*

GRANT HAD REMAINED IN the hospital for nearly a week, and Rena had been at his side nearly every moment, bringing ice chips, sneaking in fast-food burgers, making sure he always had a heated blanket. The only time she'd left him was on Rosie's first day of school. Even then, she'd been in near-constant contact, texting pictures of their girl, backpack straps over her shoulders and lunchbox in one hand, standing beneath the big letters that spelled out Sentinal Lane Elementary.

Once Grant came home, his recovery had taken far longer than anyone, even Dr. Stewart, had anticipated. Grant had missed weeks of work, but thanks to Rena, who'd set up a temporary work station in the family room, he hadn't fallen too far behind, even conducting Skype conferences with a few new clients. Strangely, his production increased while working at home, despite having Rena around to distract him with homemade cookies and fresh soups, the occasional back rub, and sweet humming as she went about her daily activities.

Several times, he'd asked if she missed working. And each time, she'd made it clear that she'd apply for a job at the hospital as soon as he'd fully regained his health and Danes assured them that Rosie was in no danger of backsliding, psychologically. If she'd seemed at all unhappy, would he have coaxed her to go back to nursing? Probably. But since she was apparently content with trying to make him fat, Grant decided not to rock the boat. Besides, he enjoyed the time they spent together, solving all the world's problems and discussing Rosie's steady progress.

His favorite time? When Rosie came in from school, flush-faced and excited to tell him all about her day. On Tuesday, Daniel Jensen had chipped a tooth while playing Keep Away on the playground; Joelle Hudson had come in on Wednesday sporting a short bob after donating a foot and a half of hair to kids with cancer; Thursday brought an author who'd taught them how to plot out a story; and on Friday, Ms. Gilmore had shown off her sparkly new engagement ring.

Rosie's nightmares about the years with Barbara were happening less often now, and she seemed happy and self-assured in her new world. He and Rena had grown more secure about Rosie's emotional adjustment, too, leaving her long enough to attend classmates' birthday parties—even those of the sleepover variety.

Visitors stopped by to see him now and then, some bearing gifts, others just sharing the latest family and office gossip. Today, after Joe Michaels delivered a mesh sack of Florida oranges to make up for infecting him with meningitis—he himself had never exhibited any symptoms, and his son had recovered quickly—Grant decided to soak up some warm sunshine, a pleasant diversion from the usually chilly weather.

It would be Thanksgiving soon, and he'd been doing his level best to stay out of the who's-hosting-dinner dispute between his mom and sisters. By rights, the family should gather here, since Rena had missed hosting several years running. But, as was her way, Rena had chosen to stay in the background, too, promising to help in any way she could once they'd made a decision. Trouble was, if they didn't make up their minds soon, the holiday would come and go, and no one would get so much as a slice of turkey.

He inhaled the crisp scent of the pines

that formed the side borders of the property. The sun would set soon, and when it did, it would take its pleasant warmth with it. Blue jays cawed from the now-leafless sugar maple, and cardinals peeped as they scavenged sunflower seeds that had fallen from the feeders. A light breeze riffled his hair, reminding him he needed to pay a visit to the barber's...even though Rena said she liked the way it curled over his collar.

Smiling to himself, Grant admitted that life was good, real good. Admitted, too, that he was one lucky man. He thought of how close he'd come, in the hospital, to losing it all...

"Grant? Are you all right?"

Rena sat at the foot of the lounge chair, her brow furrowed with concern.

"I'm fine. Why?"

"You looked, I don't know, *pained*, for lack of a better word."

"Just thinking," he said. "About how much has changed since this time last year."

Rena nodded as a squirrel raced across the yard, cheeks all puffed out, and climbed the oak tree. The amusing sight broke the moment of tension.

"They built a nest up there while you were gone," Grant said. "Bet it's chocked full of nuts. And sunflower seeds."

Rena laughed. "The squirrels eat more bird food than the birds." She patted his shin. "Are you warm enough?"

"Yup. Turned out to be a real nice day."

"It's good you can enjoy this weather. Normally, you'd be trapped in the recirculated air at the office."

"I guess a little meningitis is good for what ails ya, after all."

"Not funny," she said. "You had me really scared. For a while there, it looked like we might lose you."

"You can't get rid of me that easily."

She stared deep into his eyes and shook her head. If he had to guess, Grant would say she was thinking something along the lines of *I don't want to get rid of you, easily or otherwise.*

"So what's for supper?"

"Meatloaf, baked potatoes and salad."

"What, no dessert?"

"Ice cream with chocolate sauce."

Rosie joined them on the deck and, sitting beside Rena, said, "What are you guys doing out here? It's almost dark."

"Oh, just talking," Rena answered. "Have you finished your homework?"

"Everything but the report about Rosa Parks."

She'd made a diorama that resembled a bus. Made a doll out of an empty water bottle, too, painting a Styrofoam ball for the head and drawing eyes, eyeglasses and a sweet smile on it.

"Did you find the yarn I left out for you to use as her hair?"

"Yup. And Grandma gave me a couple of quilt squares for her dress and coat. All I need now is to figure out how to make her a hat."

In the past, Grant might have called a conversation like this small talk. And, in the past, he would have loathed it. Lately, though, ordinary banter had taken on new meaning, and he treasured every word between Rosie and Rena, between Rena and his mom, between all of the women in his life and himself. No words were more precious, though, than those spoken by Rena, especially when night had settled and they were alone in their room.

Their room. He was tempted to board up the guest room, to guarantee she'd never sleep there again.

"Shouldn't we go inside? It's almost dark," Rosie said again.

Rising, Rena said "You make a good point. I need to set the table for supper, anyway."

Rosie beat her to the door. "You coming, Dad?"

"In a minute. There won't be very many more days like this before Old Man Winter shows up."

His wife and daughter exchanged a knowing glance.

"I'll call you when the food is on the table, then. Need anything in the meantime?"

"I'm good, thanks."

When the door closed behind them, Grant stared at the dimming sky. A full moon tonight, he noticed. Later, when it was full-dark, there would be stars, too. Maybe even a Venus sighting. Feeling rested and relaxed, he let his hand dangle from the chair, as his eyes closed.

"Grant?"

He startled. Had he dozed off?

"Mom. Sheesh. You scared me half to death."

"What are you doing out here, all alone in the dark?" Tina asked.

"What are *you* doing, walking around all alone in the dark?" he shot back.

"Rena invited me to supper."

Instead of heading right inside, as he expected her to, she took a seat beside him.

"I'm proud of you, son," his mother said.

"Proud? Why? I owe my recovery to Rena. And medical science."

"Not that. I'm proud of you because you're working hard to repair things between the two of you. I know it hasn't been easy, but it does my old heart good to see you two together again. And Rosie… That little girl has come such a long way, and the pair of you are largely responsible for that."

"Rena gets most of the credit. Her patience is infinite. Especially with me."

"That's a long sight from where you were a few years ago."

He met her eyes. "What do you mean?"

"When you were stomping around like a raging bull, snorting accusations and blame until she felt the only way to help you heal was to leave."

Leaning forward in the deck chair he said, *"What?"*

"No disrespect intended, but you behaved abominably. Never, not once since you were born, was I ashamed of you. Until you drove Rena away."

"I need to go help get the roast on the table," he said, standing. What better way to avoid her disapproving stare?

Tina put herself between him and the back door. "You're my son, and I love you. Which is why I never said anything about this before. You were such a mess that I was afraid if I told you how I really felt, you'd go completely off the deep end!"

Grant had thought he'd buried all that. Evidently, he'd thought wrong.

"You realize, don't you, that it was *my* idea to turn Rosie's room into an office for you?

Rena and I…we were at our wits' end. You were suffering, inconsolable and taking your misery out on the one person who loved you most. I thought maybe if you didn't have all the physical reminders of Rosie to deal with every time you passed her room, you could get on with your life…your life with *Rena*."

"It's ancient history now, Mom. Rena and I…we're working things out."

"Really?"

"Really."

"So she knows you don't blame her anymore."

She couldn't have stunned him more if she'd slapped him.

"Well?"

"I haven't said it in so many words, but I think she knows how I feel."

"You *think* she knows?"

"Mom, please. I'm whipped. Can't this wait?"

"Until when?"

He started walking toward the house, intent on putting this sorry subject behind him. Where it belonged.

"Honestly, Grant. You're lucky Rena doesn't hold grudges. I hope you know that."

"You're right." He spun around. "And I do know that. I know how lucky I am that she came back to me. Lucky she puts up with me. Lucky she was here when I got sick. Lucky she's the kind of woman who'll stick with me, even when stupid, hurtful things come out of my mouth."

Grant felt guilty, taking his frustrations out on his mom. So he slung an arm over her shoulders and gave her a sideways hug.

"I'm lucky to have a mother like you, too."

She waved the compliment away. "Oh, you…" She gave his cheek a maternal pat. "I'm getting chilly. Let's go inside." She paused as she reached for the door handle. "And by the way, I love you, too."

CHAPTER TWENTY-ONE

"So," Grant asked his mom, "have you and the girls figured out who's hosting Thanksgiving this year?"

"Actually, now that you mention it, we have."

Rena scooped up a spoonful of ice cream. "Let me guess—Anni's house, because her dining room is bigger than Tressia's."

"Wrong! We put our heads together the other day and decided that since you missed the festivities for a couple of years, you should do it." Tina sipped her water. "Besides, you're a better cook than all three of us put together."

"I'm flabbergasted. And flattered. Are you sure? I know how much you and your daughters love to host."

"We've all roasted our fair share of turkeys. And I'll still bring my famous green bean casserole, so I'm a happy cook."

"Hey, Grandma?" Rosie piped up. "When we finish dessert, will you come to my room and read with me until it's bedtime?"

"I'd love to, but we should help your mom with the dishes first."

"No, you guys go ahead. Grant can help for a change."

"For a change? I clear the table nearly every night!"

"Nearly isn't nearly good enough," she joked.

For weeks, she'd wondered how to tell him. *When* to tell him. She'd been about to broach the subject in the backyard earlier, before Rosie had come outside. Rena knew it had to be tonight. She just had to get him to herself.

Tina had gone home and the dishes were done when she pulled out a kitchen chair and said, "Grant, sit down."

"Uh-oh. I don't like the sound of this."

"Hush, and let me talk."

"Yes, ma'am."

He'd been saying that a lot lately. Hopefully, he'd say it again in just a few minutes.

"Do you remember what I asked you that night, when you were…upset?"

"You mean the night I bawled like a schoolgirl?"

"I wouldn't put it that way, but yes, that night."

"As I recall, you asked me to forgive you."

Rena couldn't believe it. Was he actually going to tell her what she wanted to hear, with no prompting from her?

"I've been going over that in my head. Over and over, to be honest. And the truth is, there's nothing to forgive. Never was. Never will be."

That surprised her and she said so.

He shrugged, as if that was the end of it.

"But, Grant, you said in plain English that you held me accountable for what happened to Rosie."

"I did. And I'm sorry. *And* I was dead wrong."

This wasn't going at all the way she'd planned it. Rena decided to try a different approach.

"It's just…what I'm trying to say is, I need to clear the air. Start fresh. Wipe the slate clean."

His eyes widened and he paled. "What are you saying, Rena? A clean slate, meaning…"

"Oh, no. Nothing like that." She hadn't meant to freak him out.

Grant's expression relaxed. "Good. Because I thought things were going really well between us." He wiggled his eyebrows and grinned.

Rena clamped her teeth together. When he looked at her that way, she was putty in his hands. He knew it, too. But tonight, *she* needed to be in control.

"I need to hear you say it. Unless of course you don't mean it. Then this whole exercise would be futile."

He leaned forward with his elbows on his knees. "Rena. Honey. Please give me a break here. Exercise? *What* exercise?"

"The clean-slate, fresh-start exercise, of course."

Grant sat back. "Oh." He drove a hand through his hair. "So let me get this straight. You want me to say I forgive you, even though I don't believe there's anything to forgive you *for*."

Could it be that he finally understood? *A gal can hope...*

"Yes."

"Okay, then. I forgive you...on one condition."

Rena's heart sank. He didn't understand, after all.

"You have to say it, too."

"Say what?"

"That you forgive me."

"For what?"

"For being unfair. For making you feel awful about yourself. For driving you out of your own home. For making you believe I hated you, when I didn't. Not even for a minute."

"Is this sounding a little *déjà vu* to you, or am I imagining things?"

"Maybe, but when a thing is right, it bears repeating. Right?"

"Grant..."

"Rena..."

He laughed, and she couldn't help but join him.

"See, here's the thing," she said. "I have something to tell you. Something really important. But before I do, I want to be sure that this whole matter behind us. You know?"

His brow furrowed. "Not really, but I'll humor you. How about this—we'll say it together. On the count of three." He held up one hand, raised his pointer finger. "One." The middle finger popped up next. "Two." And then, the ring finger. "Three."

"I forgive you," they said together.

"There. Slate's wiped clean, the air is cleared, and we can start fresh. Satisfied?"

Rena still wasn't sure he'd meant it.

"Well?" he said.

"Well what?"

"This big important thing you want to tell me—what is it?"

Now that she had him where she wanted him—sort of—Rena was tongue-tied.

Finally, she took a deep breath. "I'm pregnant."

"You're…you're what?"

"You heard me. I'm having a baby."

He got to his feet, pulled her up with him. "Seriously?"

"Seriously."

"When?"

"May. Around the time of Rosie's birthday."

He gathered her into his arms and pressed kisses to her forehead, her cheeks, her eyelids, her chin.

She laughed. "You're happy about this, then..."

"Happy? You're kidding, right?" Picking her up, Grant whirled her around, and when he set her down again, he kissed her. Kissed her like her meant it. Kissed her the way he had before Rosie's disappearance.

"We need to go wake up Rosie."

"Why?"

"Because," he whispered, his lips touching hers, "I feel like celebrating. As a family."

Rena melted against him and memorized the moment. For some reason, the image of the Fenwick Island lighthouse came to mind, exactly the way it had looked in her rearview mirror as she left the cottage the day he called to tell her Rosie had been found. Back then, it had reminded her of the separation between her and Grant. Now, it only reminded her of all those weary sailors it had safely guided to shore.

Grant was her lighthouse, her safe harbor.

Rosie bounded into the room, grinning. "Mom…Dad…what's going on?"

"Sit down, kiddo," Grant said. "Your mom and I have something to tell you. Something we think will make you very happy."

Rena listened as Grant explained that soon, Rosie would become a big sister. And as she watched her daughter's eyes light up with anticipation and joy, she realized that her lighthouse analogy no longer fit the situation.

Lighthouses, more often than not, were lone structures, built on islands.

She wasn't alone anymore. Soon, their little family would grow, and together, they'd shelter one another.

Forever.

* * * * *

*Don't miss THE MAN SHE KNEW,
the first book in Loree Lough's
BY WAY OF THE LIGHTHOUSE
miniseries, and keep an eye out
for book three in 2018.*

Get 2 Free Books,

Plus 2 Free Gifts—

just for trying the Reader Service!

Get 2 Free Books,
Plus 2 Free Gifts—
just for trying the Reader Service!

YES! Please send me **The Hometown Hearts Collection** in Larger Print. This collection begins with 3 FREE books and 2 FREE gifts in the first shipment. Along with my 3 free books, I'll also get the next 4 books from the Hometown Hearts Collection, in LARGER PRINT, which I may either return and owe nothing, or keep for the low price of $4.99 U.S./ $5.89 CDN each plus $2.99 for shipping and handling per shipment*. If I decide to continue, about once a month for 8 months I will get 6 or 7 more books, but will only need to pay for 4. That means 2 or 3 books in every shipment will be FREE! If I decide to keep the entire collection, I'll have paid for only 32 books because 19 books are FREE! I understand that accepting the 3 free books and gifts places me under no obligation to buy anything. I can always return a shipment and cancel at any time. My free books and gifts are mine to keep no matter what I decide.

262 HCN 3432 462 HCN 3432

Name	(PLEASE PRINT)	
Address		Apt. #
City	State/Prov.	Zip/Postal Code

Signature (if under 18, a parent or guardian must sign)

Mail to the **Reader Service**:
IN U.S.A.: P.O. Box 1867, Buffalo, NY. 14240-1867
IN CANADA: P.O. Box 609, Fort Erie, Ontario L2A 5X3

* Terms and prices subject to change without notice. Prices do not include applicable taxes. Sales tax applicable in NY. Canadian residents will be charged applicable taxes. This offer is limited to one order per household. All orders subject to approval. Credit or debit balances in a customer's account(s) may be offset by any other outstanding balance owed by or to the customer. Please allow 4 to 6 weeks for delivery. Offer available while quantities last. Offer not available to Quebec residents.

Get 2 Free Books,
<u>Plus</u> 2 Free Gifts -
just for
trying the
*Reader
Service!*

Get 2 Free Books,
Plus 2 Free Gifts—
just for trying the
Reader Service!

♦HARLEQUIN®

SPECIAL EDITION